D0426628

my best friend,
the Atlantic Ocean,
and
other great bodies
standing between me
and my life with

Giulio

by Jane Harrington

For my Jonny

~

Cataloging-in-Publication

Harrington, Jane.
My best friend, the Atlantic Ocean, and other great bodies standing between me and my life with
Giulio / by Jane Harrington.
      p. ; cm.
ISBN 978-1-58196-070-9
Ages 12 and up.—Sequel to: Four things my geeky-jock-of-a-best-friend must do in Europe.—
Summary: As a class assignment, Delia keeps a journal and records her life and her fantasies about
the Italian exchange student Giulio, who also happens to be Brady's boyfriend. And, oh, by the way,
Brady is Delia's best friend.
1. Teenage girls—Juvenile fiction. 2. Best friends—Juvenile fiction. 3. High school students—
Juvenile fiction. [1. Teenage girls—Fiction. 2. Best friends—Fiction. 3. High school students—
Fiction.] I. Title. II. Author.
PZ7.H23815 My 2008
[Fic] dc22
OCLC: 174504758

Published by DARBY CREEK Publishing
7858 Industrial Parkway
Plain City, OH 43064
www.darbycreekpublishing.com

Printed in the United States of America

2 4 6 8 10 9 7 5 3 1

978-1-58196-070-9

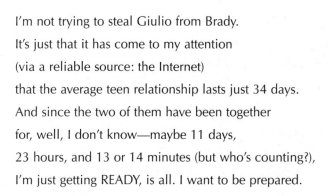

I'm not trying to steal Giulio from Brady.
It's just that it has come to my attention
(via a reliable source: the Internet)
that the average teen relationship lasts just 34 days.
And since the two of them have been together
for, well, I don't know—maybe 11 days,
23 hours, and 13 or 14 minutes (but who's counting?),
I'm just getting READY, is all. I want to be prepared.

Being prepared can't be a BAD thing,
or else it wouldn't be the official Girl Scout motto.

One way I am prepared:
I now know EXACTLY how to pronounce his name.
The Italian <u>G</u> is pronounced like a <u>J</u>

when it's before an e or an i.
The Italian i is always pronounced ee.
The Italian u is always pronounced oo.
So you say, quite fast and Italiany: Jee–oo–lee–oh.
Lee gets the most feeling.

Although the oo would definitely do a better job
of describing MY personal feelings.

So far, when I've talked to Giulio,
I've avoided actually using his name, so I don't mess up.
Now I am ready, though, since I have studied it.
(And "I" and "studied" rarely appear in the same sentence.)
I looked up pronunciations in that Italian phrase book
Brady used during her trip to Europe,
and I practiced in front of the mirror.
Perhaps I will make a career of being an Italian language expert.

I may have to know how to pronounce
more than five letters, however.

But that's okay!
Giulio will teach me to speak fluent Italian,

when we are someday married
and living in the Italian countryside,
where the sunflowers grow.
I think it's called Provence.
Or maybe the Riviera.
Or is it the Serengeti?

Well, he'll teach me Italian geography, too,
I'm sure.

Anyway!
When I see him, I'll say, softly,
"How has your first day
in an American high school been, Giulio?"
Or maybe I should say it loudly,
so everyone in the hall will see that I, Delia,
know the Italian exchange student SO well
that his name just ROLLS off my tongue.

Problem: It's last period,
and I haven't run into him ONCE today.

Brady told me at lunch that she thinks

he could be hanging out in the upperclass-people halls,
since he is a little older than we are.
But—CALL THE NEWSPAPERS!—I have figured out
something that Brady has NOT. And this is no small matter.
It may APPEAR that I am the brighter of the two us,
but Brady is really the brains of our little partnership.
Actually, of our whole class.

And she has been ever since she skipped a grade
back in elementary school.

Which means that, YES,
she is also younger than I am.
By a YEAR, in fact, which has a way of
making me get the urge to punch her sometimes.
But, of course, I wouldn't do that.
She's a lot stronger than I am.
There's also the matter of her being my best friend.
And you don't go around punching your best friend.

Even if she IS going out
with your future husband.

Since, after all,
she doesn't know
he's your future husband.
And you certainly
can't TELL her,
since that would be kind of rude,
seeing how she's
going out with him.

So, where was I before I lost
the entire point of what I was saying?

Oh yeah! I had figured out something Brady had NOT.
The something: There ARE no upperclass-people halls.
In the part of the building that has the middle school,
there are 7th and 8th grade halls,
but in the high-school wing
the halls seem to be divided by subject.
So even though Brady and I are freshman,
we are mixing and mingling with sophomores, juniors, etc.

Getting back to my dilemma, though . . .
maybe it's just safer to say: "Hello, Giulio."

Or is that too musical with those ending-o's?

And, anyway, it should be a question—not a statement.

That way he can answer in his <u>molto</u> <u>buono</u> accent.

<u>Molto</u> <u>buono</u> means "very good."

I also know that <u>arrivederci</u> means "goodbye."

Brady taught me these things.

She is a big help to me

as I prepare for my new Italian life.

Which doesn't seem right somehow.

But, oh well.

Oh, I'll just make it a SHORT question.

Like: "Hey, have you seen Brady?"

Which is very casual-hip and

oh-yeah-you're-my-friend and all that, and also very . . . .

DUMB, since it doesn't even include his name,

which was the total point of all my practice.

Okay, THIS is the final version:

"Hey, Giulio, have you seen Brady?" PERFECT.

Unless, of course, he's WITH Brady,

which is kind of likely.

I think I'm cracking under the pressure of all this waiting.
Or else it's the pressure of this 100-minute
(that's over an HOUR) English block.
The class is taught by one of those military sorts
who has given up on retirement
to become a teacher-and-commander.
It's a mystery to me why anyone would choose
to be here when they could be, well, anywhere.

Perhaps their pets refuse to stay in formation.
Or they find the rows of desks comforting in some way.

His name is Colonel Jordan,
and he's patrolling the aisles right now.
No one is saying one word.
Which is VERY strange for this group of humans,
let me tell you.
If I ever become a teacher,
I will call myself Sergeant Delia
so people listen to me.

Is that impersonating an officer?
I better look into that.

After standing erect and lecturing for a solid hour,
the Colonel wrote on the white board, in purple letters:
POETRY JOURNAL RULES: WRITE POETRY.
(Which is only one rule,
but no one seems to want to point that out to him.)
Apparently we are writing in these "poetry journals"
at the end of each class block, all quarter.
We're supposed to "freely experiment with forms."

And he says he isn't going to read them. Ever.
Which made all of us stare at him for a while.

He went on to say that the journal grade
is based on whether or not
we are actually, physically writing poetry.
But since I know BUPKIS about writing poetry,
I'm just dividing my writing into a repeating pattern
that is intended to LOOK like poetry to anyone
(for instance, the Colonel)
who is passing by my desk.

I feel like Sonya Sones,
only without the talent.

Today, I've been counting off 8 lines and then 2 lines
for each stanza—if that's what these things are called.
I wonder if the word "stanza" is actually Italian.
It ends in a vowel and that seems
to be a common Italian THING
from what I am noticing—<u>molto</u>, <u>buono</u>, <u>arrivederci</u>, etc.
Wait a minute . . . this is very odd . . . .
am I having an intellectual curiosity about something?

Maybe this global-love-interest-thing is GOOD for me!
Perhaps my GPA will go up.

The Colonel just walked by
and smiled at me approvingly.
Even though what I am writing
is really just brain blabber.
So, I guess my plan is working. Excellent!
Except my arm is becoming numb
from all the writing.
Thankfully, I only have this subject every other day.

Why am I going on about English, of all things?
I still have an important decision to make.

It'll be . . . (drum roll, please) . . . "Hi, Giulio!"

Short, sweet, safe.

When I get sprung here, I'll go down the hall to that

mega-smart English class where Brady is.

Maybe he's in that class. Which would be SO not fair

that I'm getting all angsty just thinking about it.

(According to <u>Bopmag</u>, teen angst is the

#2 problem for teenagers in America today.)

(I can't remember what #1 is, but if it has something to do with

your best friend dating your future husband, I've got that, too.)

But, HOLD ON NOW . . .

Since English is not Giulio's first language,

he couldn't be in a brainiac class!

He should be in a regular English class!

With SLUGS! Like ME!

(Oh, now I remember. Poor self-esteem

is the #1 teen problem in America today.

Got that covered, too, I guess.)

OMG!!

He just walked in!!

And he's handing the Colonel a note!

I think he's in this class!!

He IS in this class!

And he's now walking toward my desk

and he . . . .

. . . just said, "Hello, Delia."

And I responded by saying, "Hi, Giulio!"

Just as I planned.

Only I said his name like this:

Goo-lee-oh.

With the feeling on the Goo,

which I pronounced the same way as the sticky kind of GOO.

What is WRONG with me???!!!

I'm now in the middle of a TOTAL TEEN ANGST FLARE-UP.

My palms are sweating and I can't BREATHE.

HEAD BUZZING must also be a teen angst symptom,

because I'm getting THAT now, too.

It's so LOUD! HELP!

Oh. That's the bell.

Arrivederci.

bad

poetry

If this room were a clock . . .
a rectangular clock . . .
(but not a digital clock,
since that wouldn't make sense)
and the front of the room were 12 o'clock,
I'd be at about 4 o'clock
and Giulio would be at about 9 o'clock.

Or, to use a Brady-ish comparison,
if the room were a baseball diamond,
and the front of the room were home plate,
my desk would be just behind 3rd base,
and Giulio would be at 1st base.
But connecting "Giulio" with "1st base"
is making me feel a little unusual.

Like when I ate shrimp and broke out in hives.
Probably just an unavoidable side effect of FUTURE LOVE.
Or GUILT over having 1st-base-kind-of-thoughts
about my best friend's boo.
But I'm not doing this on purpose!!
And even if I were, I'm not actually DOING anything.
My immediate goal is to be JUST FRIENDS with him.

Though I've never experienced it myself, I'm told
it's possible to be JUST FRIENDS with a boy-type person.
I know I tend to fall for all guys I, uh, meet, but that doesn't
mean I'm "obsessed with the opposite sex," as Brady says.
My ancestors were Greek and Brazilian,
so it may just be a cultural thing.
We're supposed to respect cultural differences, right?

Brady, on the other hand,
has been in close contact with boys for years—
and when I say "close contact," I do mean it,
because she plays sports with them—
but somehow, unexplainably,
she has never, ever gone
beyond being JUST FRIENDS.

Even with some majorly sweaty kinds of encounters
(picture soccer, if you dare),
she has not had an, uh, out-of-bounds kind of interest in ANY guy.
Not ONE.
Until now.
NOW, when I've come face-to-face with my destiny.
(Wiiiiiiish.)

So WHAT if I put her up to it?
On that night before she left for Europe,
when I wrote on her hand with my Sharpie pen:
MEET A CODE-RED EURO-HOTTIE,
I never in a zillion years thought she would actually DO it,
much less bring one home and keep him to herself.
Oh, what a selfish, selfish girl.

From where I sit, I can see his
dark brown hair, straight and pulled into a ponytail
at the back of his neck, swishing just a little bit
each time he starts a new line in his own journal.
Brady says he's an artist, so maybe he's sketching.
Or he could be "mimicking the style of e. e. cummings,"
as the Colonel has suggested we do.

We studied e. e. cummings today, and though I have
a couple of burning questions about this poet,
I am still intimidated by the military leadership of this room
and worry that if I say the wrong thing
I will have to do 75 push-ups,
or I will be sent to the stocks.
(I don't know what that means, actually.)

Here are the couple of things
I'm wondering about e. e. cummings:
Did he get points off for capitalization errors
every time he wrote his name on his homework?
And . . .
when he was a little kid and went to the zoo,
did he think the chimps all knew his name?

I'm sure, too, that other people in my class
have similarly fascinating questions in mind,
but there is still very little noise coming out of this room.
The only one who spoke up today was Shakita,
who sits in front of me, and recited—
even though she wasn't asked to—
a line from an e.e. poem the Colonel had written on the board.

"'he sang his didn't,'" she read slowly,
pausing after the "didn't."
"'he danced his did,'" she finished,
with a special emphasis on the "did."
And then she asked the Colonel,
"So, what did he do? Cut words out of
magazines and throw them in the air?"

We all just stared at her, then at the Colonel,
wondering how he would react to this insubordination.
But he just said, "Interesting. Does anyone else share her view?"
And he started looking around, trying to make eye contact
with SOMEONE, but we were all averting our gazes—
to walls, ceiling, floor, ants marching along the baseboards,
the flagpole out the window, our cuticles, etc.

Just as he was reaching for his grade book
to probably begin calling on us randomly,
Shakita piped up again and said,
"Zher view. Like 'pleasure' minus the 'pleh.'"
So we all went back to staring at her.
"Zher view?" the Colonel repeated.
"Yes, 'zher' view," she said.

He looked us over, again,
in a fairly baffled way,
so we all returned to the gazing-around activity.
It was then that I began imagining
that I could see these gazes of ours,
criss-crossing the space between us like laser beams
or maybe strands of silk from a spider.

Well, like silk from a spider,
only not from its butt,
which I think is the actual case in nature.
Clearly an argument
for remaining indoors as much as possible,
and one I will try next time my dad is
trying to shoo me away from The O.C. reruns.

ANYWAY.
The longer we sat there, looking around,
the more—in my highly creative mind—the room filled up
with these shimmery strands,
tying all of us together into a wild jumble,
with—very conveniently—desks 9 o'clock and 4 o'clock
locked in a Tetris-like embrace.

It was just about then in my mind-wanderings
that Shakita piped up again.
(OKAY, it was a LITTLE bit after,
but I'm NOT writing stuff like
that in a school journal,
even IF the teacher says
he's not reading it.)

"You asked if anyone shares 'her' view," Shakita said,
"and I'm just more comfortable with gender-neutral pronouns."
Not understanding a bit of that, I drifted back into my PG-13 web.
(Thoughts which I KNOW are wrong to have
about my best friend's boyfriend,
so there's no need to point that out,
thank-you-very-much.)

Uh, who am I talking to in all these parentheses?
AAAH! I must have those little devil-angel arguers
hanging out on my shoulders!!
GET OFF!!! I'm swatting at you!!
(In my mind, luckily.)
The angel just fell off.
Oh. Darn.

To get back to the story, the Colonel said to Shakita, "Explain."
And though one part of me (think: long red tail)
wanted to think about you-know-who,
the other part of me (the winged part)
was curious about what Shakita was getting at.
(WHAT is HAPPENING? Inquisitive thoughts, tiny beings
on my shoulders? It's INSANE being me right now.)

"I'd just rather people use 'zher' instead of 'her,'
when referring to me," Shakita said, with a confident 'tude,
as if she weren't in a military academy.
(Which she isn't, of course, but you know what I mean.)
"And also 'zhe' instead of 'she.'
It's more open-minded," she added.
Uh, I mean, <u>zhe</u> added.

The Colonel looked SERIOUSLY confused now
and began his room-scanning again,
which began our gaze-averting again,
so I began my day-dreaming again,
until I was interrupted AGAIN,
but this time by the voice of . . .
Giulio.

"I am, eh, in agreement with this Shakita," he was saying,
Which caused our leader to look even MORE confused.
"You want me to call you 'zhe' also?" he asked Giulio.
And though many people in the class chuckled at this,
I, being the open-minded person I am,
nodded toward Giulio in a supportive way
and said to the Colonel, "I, too, want to be called 'zhe.'"

And then Giulio glanced at me kindly,
but also with an expression
that one might give to a visitor
from a planet outside our solar system.
And then he said to the Colonel,
"I meant I am agreeing
with Shakita's opinion of the poet."

"I knew that!" I said, WAY too perkily.
And thinking this to be the perfect time to
relocate my life to a new city,
I darted out of the room
with Taz-like swiftness,
leaving the Colonel announcing to the class,
"Zhe left zher backpack here!"

Not really, of course. I am OBVIOUSLY still in this room.
Just hanging out, trying to express my feelings today
in these seven-line stanzas of faux poetry.
(Why seven? Why NOT?)
Even writing faux poetry, though, is a MAJOR chore for me,
since I am so, so very poetry-challenged.
Is that a handicap, I wonder? Maybe I can get special services.

Shakita has just passed me a note.
It says:
"Gender Neutral Alliance meets on Thursday after school."
As Brady's grandmother would say: <u>OY</u> <u>VAY</u>.
Which is probably a Yiddish cussing phrase,
Making it quite PERFECT
to express the types of feelings I'm, uh, feeling.

PERFECT, like the Colonel says
this other e. e. cummings poem is.
The one that's also on the board, and is called "1(a."
There are less than twenty letters in the entire thing,
perfectly arranged so each line is complete
but for one minor thing: words.
As in, the type you find in a dictionary.

The Colonel claims the poem
"highlights the
theme of oneness
in every possible way."
And that it's brilliant.
Which gives me
real hope that even I . . .

c
ou
ld b
e vi
ewed a
s br
illian
t on
e da
y.

Today we read a few of Shakespeare's sonnets, so I will try to write some of this entry sonnet-style. Only without that ABBA and ACDC rhyming stuff. I'll also be leaving out the thees and thines and thighs, or w/e. And, of course, actual poetic SKILL will be missing. But otherwise it will be very much like Shakespeare, I'm sure.

I really liked this one sonnet we read today. It was in our lit book, and the last line is: "Love's fire heats water, water cools not love." I don't know WHAT it means, but it sounds AWESOME. That sonnet is called "CLIV," and I also don't know what THAT means. Another sonnet we read was called "LIX," which is a pretty weird name, too. Shakita seems to know a lot about Shakespeare, so maybe I'll ask her what's up with the names. I mean, I'll ask zher. Hold on . . .

Hm. Shakita says "CLIV" is not a word—it's the number 154. And "LIX" is the number 59. Which sounds pretty bogus to me, but zhe seemed pretty confident about that. Shakespeare sure was a mystery. Such a mystery, in fact, that Shakita thinks he was a woman. There's this whole theory about it, apparently, which zhe explained in great depth during this class block. It involved a woman writer named Elizabeth who was a daughter of an Earl, and also the wife of an Earl.

"Many people have analyzed the writing of Shakespeare and agree that it's too good to have been written by a slacker who went to school for only a couple of years," zhe said. "And since women writers would not have been allowed to publish anything in that oppressive society, there is good reason to believe an educated woman could have written the works of Shakespeare."

There was a little debate going on in class for a while about this, with some people liking the idea, but most taking the position that they couldn't accept it on the grounds that it would, quite obviously, RUIN the movie Shakespeare in Love for them.

"So what's up with the Earl thing?" I asked, trying to slightly change the direction of the conversation, since Shakita was starting to get a little intense. "I guess it was a really popular name, huh? Or else this Elizabeth was married to her dad, which would be e-w-w-w."

This produced a bit of staring in my direction, until Shakita turned around and said, "It's a British title, like a duke or a count."

I intently looked at my lit book at that moment, figuring it was a good time to do some studying—of Giulio, out of the corner of my eye. I was hoping to find that he had been napping throughout this little exchange. But, no, he was looking at me. With a patient expression. Like you might give a very good-natured mentally challenged person.

"This is all very interesting, really, thank you for the input and enthusiasm," the Colonel said to the class. "But we'd better get back to reading his—"

"'Zher' would work better than 'his' in this context, especially given the debate, don't you think?" Shakita asked him.

The Colonel looked a little flustered, but said, "Okay, then, we better get back to reading zher sonnets—"

"Wouldn't it be 'zhis?'" someone in the class asked Shakita.

"No, 'zher' is in place of 'him' or 'her,'" zhe answered.

Other people in the class had more questions about the zh-words, and they were asking Shakita directly, which—I could tell—was starting to miff the Colonel, judging by some throat-clearing that was getting more intense as the conversation lengthened. Finally, when it sounded like he was getting TB, everyone jolted their heads in his direction, seeming to suddenly remember he was the teacher. He hasn't been in a very good mood since all that, and since he's nearing my desk at this moment, I think I better get to my sonnetizing:

Lots of sonnets are about LOVE, LOVE, LOVE.
(Now I hear that Beatles song in my head.)
Which is another reminder of the
Circumstances of my immediate life.
Sonnets also make me think of that movie
Shakespeare wrote, called <u>Romeo</u> <u>and</u> <u>Juliet</u>.
Juliet was 14, just like me, and
She could not be with her sweet Romeo,
As I cannot be with my sweet Giulio.
Only she had it a little better,
Because Romeo knew she loved him, and
He loved her back with all his heart and soul.
    They're not actually alive at the end,
        But you can't ask for everything, now can you?

A tiny baseball player on my desk
Has just nodded his agreement with me.
Last week, the Colonel—seeing how many
Of my classmates were having trouble
Getting much of anything written—
Suggested we find something to inspire us.
Some little chachka (as Brady's grandma
Would call a thing that is, um, purposeless.)

So I brought in this little baseball player.
He is a bobblehead doll, so when my
Desk jiggles, he nods at me.
His little baseball cap is red and white.
  I got him free at the stadium in D.C.
  They were giving them out at the baseball game.

LUCKILY, the Colonel just sat down to grade papers, so I'm going to stop sonneting for a while. I'm SO not exerting all that effort when he's not watching. I'm not into that over-achievement thing, after all. I mean, there could be a limited amount of achievement in my body, and what if I use it all up before I reach, say, 17? THEN what?

So, back to the baseball game . . .

Brady was very surprised I said yes when she and Giulio asked me to go with them.

"It's about time," she said. "I've been asking you to go to a game for FIVE months, and you've always said you had 'important things to do,' like, I remember once you said you had to scrub the algae off the walls of your dad's fish tank. And once you told me you really wanted to go, but there was a Gilligan's Island festival on TV. And how 'bout that time you said you were afraid the baseballs might be injected with hantavirus as

31

part of a terrorist plot? And then there was the nap, the hair highlighting, the dusting of your mom's chess pieces, and—"

"Well, those things CAN be important," I said, hoping to head her off before she got to the excuse about needing to rid my entire yard of worms.

I just don't understand what all the excitement is about baseball, though. Besides, of course, the Dippin' Dots stand at the stadium, which is WAY cool. I recognized a guy from school scooping the Dots, and in a prior life I would have spent a lot of time talking to him about stuff, and maybe getting his screen name or something. But now that I am in a serious relationship-to-be, I am no longer playing the field.

Hey! "Playing the field" is, I think, a sports-related idiom! Which is alarming in TWO ways: (1) that I actually NOTICED this . . . I continue to amaze myself with my sudden surge in intellect . . . and, (2) that I actually NOTICED this. Which sound like the same things—and, of course, ARE the same things—but what I mean is that it is unusual for me to notice that something is an idiom AND it's unusual for me to notice that a saying COMES from something . . . especially SPORTS.

Where WAS I anyway? Oh, yeah, at RFK Stadium, watching a baseball game.

Giulio seemed to really like the game and also seemed to

enjoy the music playing in the stadium. He knew the words to every song that was played—"We Will Rock You," "We Are the Champions," "All Star," "Hey Ya." I have noticed, in fact, that he knows the words to almost every song that ever comes on the radio. I asked him about this, and he said all Italian kids listen to American music and sing along, but they don't know what any of the words mean. They just sing them.

When Giulio and I get married, and I meet all his friends, I will tell them what all the words to all these songs actually MEAN. I will be their American connection to music and EVERYTHING.

Hm. I guess we're not actually going to be able to get married for some years, considering our ages and that we don't live in those young-marrying times, like Romeo and Juliet (fictionally) did. We'll have to date for, like, YEARS, I guess. Which could be a challenge, since he will be returning to Italy at the end of the school year, and there will be a very large ocean between us.

Problems, problems. I'll deal with that later.

Speaking of problems, I just don't think Brady and Giulio are facing the fact that their relationship is almost over. It is, by my count, day 18. That gives them, on average, 16 days left, but they're just having a good old time, acting like all is fine, and that no end is near. So, I better stay close by, to help them out when they are surprised by this. (That's what friends are for.)

Unfortunately, this will involve some more baseball experiences, since Brady's fall ball season is starting tonight, and Giulio has said he is planning to go to all her games. So, I told him, okay, I would go and show him where the field is and sit with him to help him understand the game and all. These are sacrifices I am willing to make. No one said life would be baseball-free.

The Colonel is circulating around the room again. I better get back to my sonneting . . .

The reason I have usually gone to
Brady's games is for purposes of
Observing some of the other players—
Her teammates all being of the boy persuasion,
And in need of observing sometimes.
But I am looking forward to this game,
Even though I don't care about that now.
You see, I have a hunch that this night'll be
A turning point for this near-expired romance.
When Giulio sees what Brady looks like
After the average baseball game:
Dirt from nose to cleat, all streaked with sweat.
   Scrapes on her legs from sliding, oozing blood.
   Not pretty. So surely my life will change now.

Today the Colonel told us that we, as a group, seem kind of stressed when we're doing our poetry journals. He thinks we may be trying too hard to create "poetry" (and he made those little air-quotation-marks with his fingers). This, he said, is probably why some of us are not producing any actual WORDS. He wasn't talking about ME—that's for sure. I am having a blab-fest. But I don't want to bring that to anyone's attention, or else I could be called upon to read from my journal. BBijn;fljhfasrhilha!!! (That was me expressing the spaz attack I had in my mind just thinking about having to read this out loud.)

I find myself actually looking forward to this class, just to write in this thing. (Well, okay, I mainly look forward to it so I can be in the same room with Giulio, but there's no rule about telling the truth in this journal.) It feels almost like a therapy session, only without a psychologist bugging you. Perhaps I will actually start keeping a real journal.

Again, I am scaring myself with thoughts such as these. Brady is the journal keeper of the two us, not me.

Or should that be 'I'?

Did I really just ask myself a grammar question?

HELP!! Who AM I??!!

Well, I'll sort that out later. Back to the Colonel . . .

He told us that we should not feel "constrained" by trying to make our poetry "fit into a structure" as we write it. That to become good writers we need to "release the words and let them flap about on the winds of our creativity." He says the best writing comes from free writing about anything that inspires, and that later we can edit the writing down to its most "vital essence." And that, he says, will result in good poetry.

Then, to emphasize this new approach to things, he picked up his purple marker and revised his "POETRY JOURNAL RULES" to: JUST WRITE!

(Which means I have, all along, been doing what he wants us to do. What a letdown. I hope this realization doesn't result in writer's block.)

So, today we are supposed to write our what-we-want-to entry, and then he will give us a minute at the end to vitalize the essence, or whatever it is he said. I will now let my words flap freely in my creativity. (That sounds weird.) Go, little words, fly away!

I went to Brady's game yesterday, as planned. And I went on and on and on and on to Giulio about what an amazing player Brady is, and how she's WAY stronger than most of those boys on her team, and that she slides head-first into bases and has no regard for how much sweat or spit or blood she's smeared with by the end of the game.

"That's so COOL," he said.

Which was not the response I was hoping for. But I didn't let it bother me. I figured that—hey—it wouldn't possibly seem so COOL when he actually saw her like that. I mean, I've seen it, and even though I'm her best friend, it's caused me to gag.

"Delia, I hope you will tell me what is going on, since this is only my second baseball game ever to watch," he said to me.

(Oh, I LOVE the way he says "Delia." I need to make a podcast of that so I can play it for myself all day long.)

"You can count on me," I said, giving his leg a little pat.

Which made me feel guilty, touching him like that, even though people touch each other like that all the time and it doesn't mean anything. And it DIDN'T mean anything, even though once I did it, it FELT like it meant something.

So . . . I immediately switched the focus back to Brady and her incredible hitting abilities. I told him to sit back and brace himself for the power-hitting, super-slugging, out-of-the-park, lights-out Brady. It may have seemed over-the-top (born of post-leg-pat guilt), but it's not really an exaggeration. At least that had always been the case . . .

. . . but that night—OPENING NIGHT—Brady did not get ONE hit the entire game. She struck out every time she got up to bat. Well, except one time, when she hit the ball, and I cheered and cheered for my bestest buddy, even though it wasn't hit very hard, because I thought it was important to be supportive. Then I realized that no one else was cheering.

"I think it was a double play," Giulio whispered in my ear. (And with that whisper—sweet, soft, Italian-guy air molecules flapped freely into my ear.) "The ball was scooped up by the, eh, second baseman, and with the force on, he tagged the base and then threw it to the first baseman," he said.

"And that's a bad thing?" I asked.

He nodded, smiling at me. But with the kind of smile you might give a hedgehog with wobbly hedgehog syndrome. (Saw a picture of that once on the Internet. Think: PATHETIC.)

"Are you sure this is only the second game you've ever watched?" I asked.

"It's not hard rules to get an understanding for," he said.

(Good-looking, Italian, AND brilliant. Too good to be true.)

(Except that he's not mine, so it's too bad to be true.)

(Or is that too good to be untrue?)

(I don't know WHAT I'm talking about.)

Even though Brady never got on base, she was still pretty

much caked with the disgusting, orange-brown dirt that covers the baseball field. She plays shortstop, which requires her to spend much of the game throwing herself face-first into the ground. I've always wondered what in the world Brady could possibly get out of that sort of activity. But then, seeing how much Giulio seemed to LIKE this grossness of Brady-the-baseball-slob, I started to think . . .

and think . . .

and THINK!

That just felt SO Dr. Seuss! Which is appropriate, since Dr. Seuss was a poet, and this is a poetry class! Hey! I think I will write about what it was I got to THINKING there at the baseball game, and I'll do it in a Seuss-ish style:

Since Giulio's not into qualities lady-like,
I will work at becoming more Brady-like!
I refuse to roll in puddles of mud,
Or cover myself in gross, smelly crud,
But maybe his fancy I can tickle
By being a person more athlet-ical!

Isn't that brilliant? (I mean the idea, but the rhymes are pretty creative, too, huh?) I will become more like Brady by becoming more athletic! Of course, saying "more athletic" implies that I have some level of athleticism, which gives the wrong impression. I am completely NOT athletic and have always been quite proud of that, actually. I mean, who wants to do all that sweating, anyway? It's gross. But if embracing sweat will help me achieve my goals in life, then I will give it a try. Since I am a focused, goal-oriented person.

I will start by joining a sports team.

If only I had the slightest idea how to do that. Maybe Shakita can help me. Zhe seems to be sort of in-the-know about after-school kinds of things. Be right back . . .

Okay, I have gotten the 411 from Shakita. I whispered to zher: I NEED TO JOIN A SPORTS TEAM, STAT! HOW DOES A PERSON GET THAT DONE AROUND HERE? And zhe turned and gave me a very strange look and started to say something, but the Colonel pointed at us, and went SHHH!

So zhe scribbled a note on a piece of paper and held it up instead. It said: OH, NO. HE DID NOT SHUSH US.

I took the same note and scribbled under that: HE DID, ACTUALLY. SPORTS TEAMS?

Zhe took the note and scribbled under that: CLUBS, DELIA, CLUBS. THAT'S WHERE IT'S AT. BUT THEY'VE BEEN TALKING UP SPORTS ON THE MORNING ANNOUNCEMENTS EVERY

DAY THIS WEEK, IF YOU'RE SET ON HONING SKILLS OF
BRUTALITY AND OVER-COMPETITIVE BEHAVIOR.

Yes!

I don't mean "Yes!" I want to be brutal or over-competitive—I
mean "Yes!" I remember, hearing those morning announcements.
It's tryouts week, apparently. How utterly convenient! Let's see if I
can remember what sports are going on . . .

- FIELD HOCKEY (I do like those little plaid skirts
  and hair ribbons, but I tried this in PE and had
  some control issues with the stick.)

- CHEERLEADING (When did that become a
  sport? Anyway, I can't even watch someone do
  the splits, much less actually TRY it.)

- CROSS COUNTRY (This apparently involves—
  get this—RUNNING MANY MILES PER DAY.
  Enough said.)

There were some others, too. Golf, maybe? Football?

Hm. I have a recollection of SOMEone saying SOMEthing
about football the other day . . .

(Dreamy transition here, to a table with me, Giulio, and

Brady hanging out at the frozen custard place.)

GIULIO: So, you do cross country running and baseball at the
same time, Brady?

BRADY: I run with the high school team to cross-train. Baseball
is my main thing, and since it's not a fall sport, I have to
play in a city league right now. Are you going out for a
sport, Giulio?

GIULIO: I am comfortable with only one sport, so I will try out
for that. It is football . . .

(Dreamy transition back to English classroom and me at my
desk, writing.)
. . . football . . . football . . . football . . .
That's it! I will play football!
Well, not PLAY. Ha-ha-ha! But (because my memory skills
are obviously fabulicious today) I have just recalled that the
sports teams are all looking for managers. Maybe I can be a
team manager for football! I don't know what a team manager
DOES, but I should be okay with it, as long as it doesn't involve
physical strength. Or organizational skills. Or math. Anyway,

Giulio obviously knows what the game is all about, so maybe he can help me. Yes! I shall need help! And when he realizes that Brady is WAY too busy for him, with all her training and cross-training, I will just be THERE.

Shakita has passed me another note. It says: FREE COFFEE IN THE STUDENT LOUNGE AFTER SCHOOL. WANNA COME?

CAN'T. (I wrote back.) TRYING OUT FOR FOOTBALL.

Then zhe wrote: VERY FUNNY. BUT, REALLY, DO YOU WANT TO COME?

The Colonel is telling us to finish up our entries and do our little vitalizing of the essence thing. Hmmm . . . how to summarize and shrinkify what I have written today . . . and get to the important essenation . . . I'll try this:

I patted Giulio on the leg,
and then he whispered in my ear
about 1st base and 2nd base.
So I wrote a poem in the style of Seuss,
and now I'm joining the football team.

That wasn't so hard. I'm getting to be quite the poetess!

Friday 9/15

Ah, more fun with flapping words!

The Colonel entertained us this afternoon with a class discussion of Henry David Thoreau and Ralph Waldo Emerson, both Massachusetts boys from some olden time when, apparently, middle names were always included when talking about people. They were also both into a non-religious religion called Transcendentalism, which had a lot to do with nature, which the Transcendentalists defined as "anything that is not me." I imagine a Transcendentalist dictionary had to have been very amusing.

"Henry David Thoreau and Ralph Waldo Emerson both went to Harvard and could be considered the American founding fathers of modern poetry," the Colonel said to us.

"And just like the founding fathers of our country," Shakita whispered to me when he said that, "they were white and male."

(Zhe's been a bit hostile with the Colonel ever since the shushing incident the other day. Obviously, zhe is not a person to be shushed with.)

Zhe raised her hand then and said to the Colonel, "I hope this doesn't seem too rude, but are we going to be studying any poets that aren't irrelevant to our current lives?"

(Shakita: 1 point.)

Judging by the gasps and then the total silence, the class obviously thought the Colonel would get mad at Shakita over her little remark. But he just smiled widely and said, "That's exactly the kind of question Mr. Thoreau would have appreciated. He encouraged people to assert individuality. His written works bluntly attacked the government of the nineteenth century and later became teachings for Gandhi, King, and other proponents of passive resistance."

(The Colonel: 1 point.)

"Then," Shakita went on, "Mr. Thoreau wouldn't mind me asking if there are any women in this poetry unit we're doing?"

(Shakita moves ahead by one.)

"We've got Emily Dickinson and Maya Angelou coming up," the Colonel said. "As stated in the syllabus.'"

(And that ties things up again, folks.)

Guess what?! I have good news! I am now the manager of the varsity football team. And let me tell you, the enormous, smelly guys on the team are very enthusiastic about this. As it turns out, several of them are in this class, and they are sitting in a clump in the back right corner of the room. They wave at me whenever I look in that direction.

The bad news: Giulio is NOT on the team. But I didn't realize this until I'd sat through a whole (very LOUD) rant by the coach about how the job takes COMMITMENT, COMMITMENT, COMMITMENT, COMMITMENT (I actually counted 14 times that he said that word during the interview) and how a manager is just as important as the players and needs to have—take note of this—physical strength, good organizational skills, and a proficiency at math. To which I nodded enthusiastically, since I had not yet figured out that Giulio (who would, of course, help me overcome these minor problems) wasn't even there.

Hm. Is a nod an actual agreement? (Mental note: Ask a smart, legal-minded person about this.)

The reason Giulio wasn't there? Well, it is very widely known (or so Brady says, but I didn't know, so how widely could it REALLY be known?) that the way we play football in the U.S. is "uniquely American," and that in Europe, soccer is actually football. Or football is actually soccer. Whichever way you look at it, though, it means that Giulio plays SOCCER.

"Well," I said, when Brady and Giulio finished explaining this confusing little fact to me, "when I'm at practice, at least I'll see you running, Brady, since the track goes around the ball fields. And soccer must practice around there, too, so I'll see you, Giulio, right?"

"Actually, cross country doesn't use the track much, Deel," Brady said. "We run across fields and through woods, mainly. Kind of where the name comes from. But you're right about soccer. They do practice out there—ON the football field, in fact."

"On the football field! Great!" I commented. "But doesn't that get kind of crowded? I think there are, like, fifty football players, at least. And they're MASSIVE. In normal-people-numbers, it's easily 120 people."

"It doesn't get crowded," Brady informed me. "Because soccer is a spring sport."

This threw me , but I quickly recovered and said, quite enthusiastically, "Well, then, Giulio, since you're sportless, would you like to try this 'uniquely American' football experience?"

"Sorry, Delia," he said (very Italianly), "but since I am going to be an artist, I have to be careful not to get injuries that will harm my hands. This football I have seen, and it is too violent for my taste. And I am morally opposed to sports that are so aggressive."

Now he tells me this. NOW, when I have committed, committed, committed to spending the next however-many weeks of my life with this team.

"So you, uh, won't even be coming to games then?" I asked.

"Sorry," he said, "I am a pacifist."

Not sure what a pacifist is—and fearing it might somehow involve pacifiers—I changed the subject immediately.

I just realized there are MORE football players looking at me from the OTHER back corner of the room. How did I not notice these guys before? They're like a small mountain range along the back wall of the room. Except Richard, that is, who I just caught looking at me, too.

I really don't get how Richard ended up on the football team. Not only is he sort of scrawny, but he also has a history of being fairly uncoordinated. I remember when we were in elementary school he used to trip over everything. Desk legs, book bags, his own feet, dust balls. Once, at my house, he got a black eye from running into the bathroom door. I remember there was this jag when he used to come over. We were in, like, second grade, and his mother would just randomly call my mother and say that Richard really wanted to "have a play date." I would be standing there making horrible faces next to my mom and shaking my head furiously, but she would ignore me and say, "Oh, sure!

Delia would LOVE to have Richard over!" And then, when he got there, he would never say a word to me. He'd just start playing computer games. Thing was, he had a way better computer at his house. I did ask him once why he came over, and he didn't seem to understand the question. Perhaps my voice doesn't penetrate his nerd shield.

Wait a minute! I think I overheard him telling someone that he's planning to be a lawyer. I'll look for an opportunity to consult with him about this issue of the football coach and the nodding.

After I finished football practice yesterday (did I really just write that?), two of those guys—I think they're linebackers, but I don't know for sure, and I don't know what a linebacker does anyway (which means I'm in deep trouble when I have to actually keep track of the game in the score book, which is one of my "commitments" apparently)—were hanging around me, getting all noisy and stuff, and one of them pounded the other one HARD on the arm, while yelling "YO, BABY!" at him.

"Whoa!" I said to the punchor. "Do you realize you just left a bruise the size of an avocado on his shoulder?"

"Really?" (It was actually the punchee who said that. Sad.)

In a past life, I think I would have overlooked that overly macho, overly physicological sort of behavior, since they are, uh, BOYS, which used to be enough of a reason to be entertained by them. But now that my future is to be spent with a pacifist artist, I can't deal with any of this. And I'm stuck with these guys every day after school.

So, then, I guess I need to try a different approach to my, uh, LIFE, and the achievement of my important goals (translation: Giulio). There are other ways I can make myself more like Brady, right? For instance, maybe I could become smart.

Okay, I could PRETEND to become smart. I could carry books around or something. Yes, that's it! I'll carry books around. And then Giulio will see me for who I really am!

I guess that doesn't make sense, since I'll actually be acting like someone else. But I don't see a need to hyper-analyze the situation.

I wonder where the library is . . .

I just held up a sheet of paper for Shakita to see with this scrawled on it: WHERE IS THE LIBRARY?

Zhe started to draw a little map for me, but then I saw out of the corner of my eye that a certain Italian was now holding up a piece of paper in my direction. It said: LIBRARY IS DOWN-STAIRS BY GYM.

Punching someone in the shoulder doesn't seem so ridiculous suddenly, since I am having a strong desire to do that to myself.

Yo, baby.

The problem with appearing smart and carrying around a book written by Jane Austen, say, is that people who are actually smart—like Brady, for instance—want to "discuss" it with you. Like, in front of a certain other person—a gorgeous male person, for instance—and you end up looking a whole lot like the OPPOSITE of smart. Take, for example, this actual conversation in my life, which occurred yesterday at my house:

BRADY: Cool, Deel, you're reading <u>Emma</u>! That's my favorite
    book.

(That's the point in the conversation when I suspected I was in for some level of embarrassment.)

GIULIO: My mother loves Jane Austen and reads her books
    over and over and never stops talking about them.

(That's the point in the conversation when I realized it would be a humiliation-fest. So I attempted to send it off on a tangent.)

ME: That's great! Having a mother and all.

(This produced chuckling from Giulio, but not from Brady, who was now in a serious-literature-discussion zone.)

BRADY: Do you know that most popular chick-lit is based on Emma? The movie Clueless is pretty much exactly that story.

ME: Now that you mention it, yes. They both are set in Beverly Hills, right?

BRADY: Uh, no. The similarities are more about the actual plot. So, when you were first introduced to Mr. Elton, did you think he was interested in Harriet?

ME: Well, yes, I suspected that all along, Brady, but ESPECIALLY prior to Mr. Rochester arriving on the scene.

(A pause.)

GIULIO: Isn't Mr. Rochester in Jane Eyre?

ME: Yes, that's right, Giulio. He's in both books. Sort of a spin-off story situation. Jane Austen liked doing that, I hear.

BRADY: But Charlotte Brontë wrote <u>Jane</u> <u>Eyre</u>.

ME: I've heard that, too, yes. Very nice angle on the subject,
Brady. Anyone up for some fries?

Eventually, Brady had to leave. She said she had to "hole up
in the cage to get her swing back before first pitch." I was afraid
to ask.

And then a surprising thing happened. Giulio didn't leave.
Our little book chat had obviously not swayed him from
respecting my intellect, because he asked—get this—if I could
help him with his homework. To which I answered, YESSSS!!!!

(I hope I didn't seem too eager.)

He needed to study for a biology test, which, admittedly,
isn't the best homework-helping scenario for me, since biology
is not my best subject.

What is my best subject, I wonder? Tough to say, since I
stink at just about all subjects. Or, at least, all subjects THIS
school seems to teach. But maybe—to cut my brain a little
slack, here—it's not an intelligence thing. Maybe it's just that I
lack INTEREST in every subject this school has classes about.
Yeah, that.

So, to make up for what I lack in the actual science area, I kept my little help session lively by running random Google searches on words from the vocab list at the end of the chapter. This produced some very unexpected results. For instance, when I plugged in the word "keratin," something altogether disgusting appeared on the screen. That's when I flipped the monitor off and said, "I think the computer may be broken."

"It's not broken," Giulio told me. "You just push this button." Then he turned the monitor back on, and a full-screen, zoomed-in image of yellow toenail fungus appeared. (I'm shuddering just thinking about it.)

There is actually a really good reason I stay away from the study of biology. I get that thing—psychosomania, I believe it's called—if I even THINK about illnesses. When I was looking at Giulio's biology book, there was this box about chicken pox on one page, and I was scratching away at my arms and legs within seconds of seeing it. I flipped to another page, and that one had a picture of a flesh-eating bacteria. So I screamed and slammed the book shut. "I think the book may be broken," I said when I recovered.

(This got another adorable little laugh out of Giulio.)

So, I've given up—for good—being smart.

I mean, pretending to be smart.

Even though the homework session was fairly worthless at

accomplishing actual, uh, homework, it was successful in another, more important way. And that is that Giulio was clearly amused by my attempts at, uh, amusing him. And—after I informed him that he was definitely ready for the big test, and we could quit—he asked me to GO somewhere with him. GO, as in go ON something. The same way you'd use the word GO with the words ON A DATE. Only it was Brady's game that he wanted to go to, so it wasn't a date, since dates don't usually involve watching a person's girlfriend play a sport. But there's no need to be all technical about that.

At the game, Brady continued striking out, which is truly weird beyond words. After the last inning, she sat down on the bleachers with us and said, "I don't get it. I don't GET it. I was slamming 'em full-on in the cage."

"What does that mean?" I asked, scooting away from her, ever so slightly, so she wouldn't take it personally (that she smelled bad and was covered with dirt).

"I was hitting the ball just fine in the practice area, Delia," she said. (A little testily, I might add.) "I'm getting my eyes checked."

"We can stop in that eye place at the mall," I suggested. "While we're shopping for my new football wardrobe."

"You don't call athletic wear a 'wardrobe,'" Brady told me (still a little testily). "And you don't even need any special clothes to manage the football team. But I'll go to the mall with you. Maybe some new socks would help me get my swing going again."

Though this was clearly crazy talk, given her recent mood, I decided to let it pass without asking any questions. I'd never been introduced to this 'losing' side of Brady before. Not very pleasant, it is. But that's okay! Best friends put up with little quirks. Especially when said quirks could, possibly, turn out to repel mondo-cutio boyfriends who will soon (in eight days, but who's counting?) reach their date-life expectancies.

While we were at the mall—specifically, standing in the sock department of Model's Sporting Goods—she explained about baseball superstitions. There seems to be a whole lot of OCD behavior going on in that sport, according to Brady. Players tend to do these ritualistic things, like taking exactly five practice swings every time they come to bat, or kicking the dirt exactly seven times, or rubbing their heads three times, etc. This is because, apparently, they're convinced that if they change ANYTHING they will ruin their game.

"Sometimes," she said, "players have to add accidental things into their routines, like if someone wipes sweat off his forehead and then he hits a home run at that at-bat, he has to always go through the sweat-wiping thing from that point on."

"Oh, I get it!" I said. "So, like, if they happen to accidentally poke themselves in the eye before they hit a triple, then they have to add that into the routine?"

"Exactly," Brady said. "My favorite is when someone scratches his butt and then gets a hit."

And then we started suggesting other things, like sneezing and nose-picking, which got us both cracking up, and thankfully got Brady out of that loser mood she was in. We were fairly out of control by the time I put farting on the list and were attracting some attention from the Model's staff.

"How do they have enough time for all that, anyway?" I asked, trying to pull myself together.

"Well," Brady said, "the players stop some of the things when they're in a losing streak, or they change what they do. Sometimes a whole team will change something together, like their socks, or pants, or something else."

I was going to make suggestions about what, exactly, "something else" could be, but I figured we better not risk getting kicked out of the store before Brady selected her new socks. Of course, Brady didn't end up getting new socks. She got all worried that her coach would get mad if she didn't match the rest of the team.

"How about a new sports bra then?" I suggested. "You don't have to worry about matching the other players with that. At least

I hope not, considering all the other players are boys. I was just going to find the rack of sports bras, myself, because I need one."

Brady started laughing again, which wasn't—in my personal opinion—a particularly funny moment.

"What's so amusing?" I asked.

"Why do you need a sports bra for managing a football team?" she asked.

"I thought I might actually start doing some of the warm-up laps with the guys," I said.

"Okay," she said, with that up-eyebrow look that means: ". . . and?"

"And I'll be running," I said. "You know, RUNNING."

Same look from her, only with the added palms-up effect, which shows you're REALLY waiting for the punch-line.

"The bra stops the bouncing," I said.

"What bouncing?" she asked.

"I bounce," I said.

"I don't think so," Brady said. "And, believe me, I know bouncing."

"You just watch," I told her. And I started jumping up and down in the middle of the sock department. "See?"

"That is not a BOUNCE," she told me. "A jiggle, maybe, but DEFINITELY not a bounce."

"This is no JIGGLE," I insisted, jumping with a level of energy that might have gotten me recruited by the basketball coach if she had been there at Model's looking at socks. "I think I may even need a medium-size bra for THIS major bouncing going on!"

Right in line with most of the other things currently happening in my life, this occurred: Giulio returned from his mission to find new shin guards. And judging by the smirk on his face, I'd say that I, again, provided him with some amusement.

Later, after I emerged from the dressing room with my (sadly, SMALL) selection (which makes me look like a nine-year-old when I am wearing it), I found Brady with her sports bra tucked under her arm (large) (large bra, not large arm) (although, her arm is kind of large) (at least compared to mine). She was tossing around a hacky sack with Giulio and looking ridiculously athletic. I may have to kill her. It would have to be a way that requires no strength, though. Like poisoning.

The Colonel has walked by my desk three times today while I've been writing, and each time he has nodded very approvingly to me. More than approvingly, he looked at me as if I were the star student in his class. Which didn't seem at all right, considering he had made the strong suggestion that we at least TRY to use some of Emily Dickinson's writing techniques, such as "unconventional broken rhyming meter" (whatever that is) in our journals today. How UTTERLY frustrating to be treated that way when you're going OUT of your way to IGNORE all parts of the lesson he's spent over an hour teaching. I may complain to my guidance counselor.

inspire

Thursday 9/21

Unfortunately, I must report that the little inspirational chachkas have now been permanently banned from the classroom. This is because of two things that happened.

> (1) People started insisting that their cell phones were inspirational chachkas; and

> (2) when the Colonel outlawed the cell-phones-as-chachkas, Beanie Babies began appearing in place of the phones.

Or, more accurately, in FRONT of the phones. Do you know that the average cell phone is completely camouflaged when it's tucked, all comfy-like, against the belly of the pink "Awareness" Beanie? I only know this because that was the Beanie Shakita brought in. I wouldn't bring in anything like that, after all! I mean, I never collected the bears. In my Beanie days, I was all about the ocean-going critters. (And Inky the Octopus does a MUCH better job of hiding a cell phone than any BEAR.)

An interesting discussion started after the Colonel announced the end of cell phones, etc. A few of the football guys started arguing that they were using the phones to text message, which was WRITING, after all, and how was that so different from writing in journals?

"Do you feel your text messages are poetic?" the Colonel asked the football guy who was the cell phone protest ringleader (haha! ring leader!). I can't remember his name, but I know he had a concussion last week from running smack into the goal posts when he was scoring a touchdown, though no one was within ten yards of him at the time. Perhaps the concussion, I started thinking, had jolted him into a higher level of intellect, because his argument about the cell phone was not sounding so bad.

"Yes, I do," he said to the Colonel.

"May I read them?" the Colonel asked.

"I guess," he answered.

The Colonel then flipped through the guy's messages, read them to himself for a few seconds, and then said, "May I share them?"

"I guess," the football player said.

So, the Colonel headed up to the board, grabbed his purple marker, and wrote this:

so boi wut up?

trifin

aiight. where u git that bama shirt?

yo! it's tight! chics checkin it out, freak.

jes some rah rah. nah mean?

fo shizzle

"What IS that?" the Colonel asked, after he had stared at it for a minute.

"It's fly, you know, sort of like rap," the football player said.

"Rap. Interesting. But what does it say?" he asked.

Feeling rather bored and wanting to add a little life to the afternoon, I raised my hand and said, "Oh, stewardess! I speak jive!"

Which is from my #2 all-time favorite movie and a line I thought all of my classmates would immediately recognize, but only a few laughed at my little fun. The rest just looked at me as if I were a lunatic, or an adult, or some other equally out-of-touch breed of human. This was reinforced when the Colonel said:

"That's from <u>Airplane</u>. One of my favorite movies. Yes, go ahead and translate, thanks."

After a very large sigh, I gave it my best shot:

What's up?

Nothing.

All right. Where'd you get that bama shirt?

Hey! It's great! Girls are looking at it, you weirdo.

I'm just kidding. You know what I mean?

For sure.

The Colonel did some serious nodding after that, and then said, "Bama?"

"That's, uh," I said, "kind of stupid-looking, or like—"

"His shirt," the football player said, pointing to the guy next to him, who had apparently been the person he was texting with.

This, of course, got things REALLY out of control.

"SO, WOULD ANYONE," the Colonel started saying at a decibel level higher than that of the room, "LIKE TO REWRITE THIS IN THE STYLE OF MAYA ANGELOU?" Which was obviously a desperate attempt to bring the focus back to what he was actually trying to teach at that point in time.

"Maya who?" the football guy asked. "Is she in this class?"

(Quite obviously, the concussion had not had the intellect-jolting effect I was thinking of.)

"Rap IS poetry," Shakita said. "Why aren't we taking it seriously? Shouldn't it be in a poetry unit?"

"Alternative poetry forms start the week after next," the Colonel said. "Page three of the syllabus."

(Another point for him. He moves ahead by one, to bring the score to 3 for the Colonel, 2 for Shakita.)

I was just trying to catch Richard's eye, but he either never looks up, or he looks down just before my eyes reach him, EVERY time. Strange. Some people are hard to figure out— they're mysteries. Or, to use a vocabulary word I have recently learned (one that means RIDDLE), they're enemas.

Not a big deal, though. I just wanted to thank him for running with me at practice yesterday. I know he could have gotten ahead, but he kept my pace. (Which, admittedly, got so slow at some points that I may have even been going back- ward.) The "warm-up lap," as it turns out, has a big stretch in the woods, and when I realized that, I was a tad bit freaked because I knew I was not going to be able to keep up with the footballers, and there I would be, ALONE!, with foxes or bears or killer rats, or those nasty monsters like in the movie The Village. (Could happen.) So, when my (so-called) teammates started zipping past me, it was really nice to find Richard there.

I was a little concerned at first that he might start tripping over tree roots or slipping on slugs, but it wasn't like that at all. He actually has a gracefulness about his running that is very natural. Like a deer, in a way. He didn't SAY anything (which is also deer-like, come to think of it), but that was fine. It gave me some time to think about my next step in the mission to be more like my best friend . . .

Having given up on trying to be athletic and trying to be smart, I was feeling like I had run out of options. But then—loping along silently next to deer-Richard—I was struck with a profound thought. Giulio, I realized, had not been at all deterred from his interest in Brady, even though he hadn't seen her get ANY hits so far at her games. Perhaps, I got to thinking, when it comes to Brady's athletic shape, maybe it is more the "shape" than the "athletic" that interests him.

And this idea inspired my new plan, which is to:

GET BOOBS.

(Ideally, two.)

I'm really just working through the details now, but I think the first step will have to be a diet. To gain weight. Though all the teen magazines would consider someone like Brady a bit on the pudge side, the truth is that she has always been a guy-magnet. She has been quite good at repelling (or being clueless about) these guys—up until now, of course—but there have been boys-aplenty chasing her around the baseball field over the years, trying to tag her out . . . if you know what I mean.

(I don't know what I mean, but I thought maybe you would.) (But I'm writing to myself, so I AM you. And I still don't know what I mean.) (NEVER MIND.)

Exercises on top of the weight-gaining diet would probably be pretty important so I can sculpt the shape I need. I don't want the new poundage to end up, uh, on my END, for instance. I'll have to do some research about that, so the weight is channeled properly into my bustline. Perhaps there's a Web site with information. On second thought, I will research this a different way. Keywords related to that particular subject might produce some very scary results online.

Shakita is holding up one of zher sign-notes. I'll be right back, after I write back. (Ooooh! Clever one!)

Okay, the note said: MEETING IN ROOM E14, VOTE FOR GENDER NEUTRAL OFFICERS.

So I wrote back, under that: I'M A MEMBER?

And zhe wrote under that: I NOMINATED YOU YESTERDAY, AND YOU WERE VOTED IN UNANIMOUSLY.

So I wrote: HOW MANY MEMBERS R THERE?

So zhe wrote: 3

At that point, I kind of happened to look over at Giulio, and he was kind of happening to look over at us, and I'm guessing he kind of happened to be reading our little note exchange. Which kind of happened to make me feel very strange because of what kind of happened on the way into class today.

You see, Shakita asked him if he wanted to join the Gender Neutral Alliance, seeing how he was all supportive during the e.e. cummings incident.

His answer: "Sorry, Shakita. Good luck with the making of your club, though. It sounds very great, but I cannot join because I am a straight person." And then he went to his seat, apparently under the impression that the Gender Neutral Alliance is about something other than . . . whatEVER it's about.

And now I'm one of the three members, so he must think . . .

I will pretend all that hasn't gone on, because it will only complicate the plans for my entire future life.

Yesterday I told Brady I wanted to start working out, and I asked her what types of exercises she does to "stay in shape."

"I do calisthenics and stretches each day," she said, "but I assume you want to work on lats, traps, and abs, so I'll focus on large muscle groups for you."

I had no idea what she was talking about, so, naturally, I nodded, figuring there might be SOME logical relationship between "large muscle groups" and "boobs."

And then she proceeded to show me the exercises, which took at least 45 minutes.

"How do you find time to do that once a day?" I asked.

"I do that set three times a day," she answered.

So, motivated by that, I'm vowing to fit exercises into my schedule every day, from now on. It'll be tough, but if Brady can do it, so can I! (That isn't even CLOSE to being true, or POSSIBLE, but it sure felt good to think it for a nanosecond.) The real question is: What can I take out of my busy schedule to make room for this new routine? The daily aromatherapy bath? My biweekly pedicure? The exfoliating scrub? Relaxing hour on Facebook? My homework?

BINGO! That's IT!

Maybe I'll take a break from the hard work on Saturday, though since Brady, Giulio, and I are going to the National Gallery of Art in the afternoon. It was so nice of Brady to include me. And I only had to ask sixteen times.

Art smart. That boy is ART SMART. I couldn't believe all
he knew about those paintings at the National Gallery. He's
been here, what? Thirty-two days and one hour (give or take a
few minutes), and he seemed to know everything about the
collection, as if it were a museum in EUROPE, or something.
Well, turns out most of the paintings are from Europe, actually,
which was news to me.

"How unexpected!" I said when I learned this. "I never
thought our 'national' gallery would have paintings from outside
our nation!"

"There would be almost nothing on the walls in the entire
west wing of the gallery if we didn't have paintings from outside
the U.S.," Brady said to me, "because most of the paintings are
from before the mid-1700s, and our nation hadn't formed yet."

"Yes, your country is such a baby," Giulio said, his irresistible
laugh echoing off the walls of the gallery. (I had an urge to leap
about and try to catch these echoing laugh bits, but I contained
myself.) "So, Brady is right about that, Delia," Giulio said.

(I just noticed something. The names "Delia" and "Giulio")

were RIGHT next to each other at the end of that last sentence. Warm fuzzies.)

Giulio seemed to be especially knowledgeable about the art from the Italian Renaissance, which (I wasn't exactly surprised to notice) includes many, many paintings of large-bosomed women.

"Sixteenth-century Italian artists made oil paints popular and sometimes mixed finely crushed glass with the paint to get a brightness they desired," he said. "Before that, they were using powdered paints mixed with egg yolks."

"What a rude awakening," Brady said when Giulio had told us a zillion other things about these artists. "I now realize how little I know about the art in my own city."

"That's where I'm really lucky," I said. "I am in touch with how little I know about the art in my own city, so I don't have to deal with any rude awakenings going on."

Feeling generally like a stick-person after fifteen minutes with the busty subjects of Raphael and Bellini, I suggested we go have a LOT of dessert. So we headed down to the café in the basement of the National Gallery and had pastries and cocoa. Extra whipped cream for me.

Seeing all the Italian paintings got me into an Italian-language-curiosity mood. So, while we munched, I started asking Giulio to teach me some words.

"So what is 'bread' in Italian?" I asked.

"Eel pony," he said. (As in, that's what I heard, but I'm knowing for sure that is not how it's actually written in Italianese.)

"And, uh, raspberries?" I asked.

"Lamb pony," he said.

Which was sounding even stranger to me, but I continued on, assuming my ears were just having some fun at my expense. (And why shouldn't they, considering the popularity of that pastime?)

"Chocolate?" I asked.

"Choc-o-lat-a," he said.

"Ooh, I like that one," I said, browsing the menu for more ideas. "Caffe latte?"

"That is already Italian," he said.

"No kidding!" I said. "How about, uh, grande?"

"That's Italian, too," he said.

"What a coincidence!" I said.

"That's not a coincidence, Deel," Brady said. "Coffee shops do it on purpose, to seem cool and European."

"I think," Giulio said to Brady, "Delia just likes to be a funny person for us."

"Yes, that's it!" I said.

Giulio is not just a primo appreciator of humor, art history, and fine paintings, he is also a REALLY good artist. I got to see his work Saturday morning when he brought his sketch pad to Brady's game. He's got this neat little series of her (and there is definitely a feel of that sixteenth-century stuff in those drawings, now that I think about it. Only, of course, Brady was wearing a baseball uniform and not flimsy garments caught in a sixteenth-century breeze.) Brady wasn't too thrilled with the drawings, though, when she saw them after the game, seeing how they were all of her swinging the bat, and she had just spent the morning striking out.

Which means the sports bra didn't work so well at changing her luck. Sitting there after that game, seeing Brady all down-in-the-dumps, I got to thinking that maybe having a boyfriend is draining the energy out of her. So I began to look for opportunities to bring up this idea in conversation. One chance came when Brady announced (after our pigging-out session at the National Gallery café) that she was going to the YMCA to work out. She was surprised, naturally, that I jumped at the chance to go with her.

"I've asked you to go to the Y with me a hundred times, and you always have excuses," she said.

But before she could begin to ramble on about me needing to floss my teeth or pluck the fuzzballs off my peacoat or pick up the leaves in my yard (one by one), I said, "I'm working on that, uh, strengthening for my, uh, football career."

This spurred an amused look from Brady.

(I am, quite obviously, good for her morale.)

At the Y, Brady and I found treadmills side by side, and after she showed me how to work the thing, we started jogging along. Though I knew this might be a bad idea, I told her to set mine at whatever speed hers was set at. Which got me winded pretty quickly, but I tried to tough it out long enough to have my little girl-to-girl talk with her. It went something like this:

ME: So, Brady, uh, you know how you aren't hitting the ball these days?

BRADY: No, Delia, I haven't noticed that.

ME: Well, you [winded pause] aren't. And I have a theory about why [winded pause] it's happening.

BRADY: But my problem is it's NOT happening.

ME: Right, yeah. This treadmill thing [panting now] is TIRING.

BRADY: It feels good, though. I need to work off that éclair I ate at the gallery.

ME: You mean [pant], the treadmill [pant] makes you LOSE
   weight?

BRADY: Uh, yes, Delia. That might even be the POINT.

   So, I decided to stop doing that immediately.
   Only I forgot to turn off the machine immediately, so I flew
off the back of it, and right into the rowing machine. Which is
made of metal, thank-you-very-much, so little birds started
twittering around my head as I lay there beside the rowers,
looking (I expect) like a large fish knocked unconscious by a
wave. The weight trainer was there in a matter of seconds,
checking out my head for bumps or bleedage.
   I could feel the eyes of many people upon me, so I stayed
very still and looked at the floor, hoping they would all get bored
and return to their machines before they had a chance to figure
out if they knew me or not. It's possible—I kept telling myself—
for a roomful of people at the local YMCA to not know me from
somewhere or another, even though my family has lived in the
neighborhood for many decades, perhaps even a century.
   "I did that the first time, too," I heard someone say, and I
looked up to see deer-Richard standing over me. "Are you okay?"
   "Yeah, I'm great!" I said, trying to leap up (and run away),

but the weight trainer told me to stay sitting for a while, and he headed off to do whatever else weight trainers do.

"He's worried you'll sue him," Richard said, when the guy had left.

Which reminded me . . .

"You're going to be a lawyer, aren't you, Richard? I'm kind of wondering if a nod is actually a legal agreement."

"I don't know," he said. "Why?"

So I explained how I nodded to the football coach, etc. "So, like, if I changed my mind, and didn't want to actually manage the football team anymore, would I be able to get out of it? Legally?"

Smiling, he said, "I'll get back to you in eight years when I'm in law school."

This was really a new side of Richard—talking, smiling. I didn't know how to react.

"But you shouldn't quit," he added.

"My reason for doing football sort of disappeared. Why are YOU on the team, anyway?" Then, thinking that might somehow be taken as an insult, I added, "I mean, you don't seem the, uh, brutal, over-competitive type."

He just shrugged and turned kind of red and didn't answer. It started getting awkward after a minute, and then he said he should probably get back to his workout.

Brady appeared next to me at that point and said, "You need some help getting up?"

I reached a hand out and let her pull me onto my feet. "Sorry to interrupt your treadmilling with my clumsiness."

"You didn't interrupt," she said. "I waited until my set was done. It's not a good idea to stop without the cool-down. Which, I guess, you figured out."

"Keep laughing, yes, very funny," I said. "Great friend you are, leaving me in a lump on the floor, all alone like that."

"You weren't alone," she said, smirking now. "Richard was there awfully fast."

"I guess he was close by," I said.

"Uh, no, he was clear across the room at the free weights, where he has been every day for the past week or so."

Which seemed weird, but whatever.

"So, are we done now?" I asked her with a very wishful expression on my face.

"I'm going to erg and then do a quick elliptical," she said.

"I don't know what that is, but please don't feel the need to explain," I said. "Is there a snack machine around? I need to pile on some empty calories."

Rolling her eyes and tutting in my general direction, she

ignored my question and stepped into the same rowing machine that had almost killed me a moment earlier.

While looking for some junk food (I found only a machine with—get this—APPLES and CARROTS), I stumbled across a scale. And guess what? I'm an entire .5 pound heavier than I was a few days ago! Yay! I'm not totally sure about this, but my bra may even feel tighter!

Brady and I decided to take a sauna before heading home. I thought that might be a good time to again try to raise my little idea about her athletic energy being drained out of her body by the presence of a boyfriend, but I couldn't figure out how to get started. I think it had something to do with the fact that it's hard to talk about anything important when you're wearing nothing but towels. So we talked, instead, about her international friends—the people she met while on her little Mediterranean cruise in the summer.

I've had a bunch of IM conversations with two of them—the girls from Lebanon, Tatyana and Noori. I didn't have any problem understanding them, which sounds really exotic and like I'm all global and languagey, but it's just that their English is GREAT. (Probably better than mine, actually).

"Tatyana and Noori will be here at the end of October," Brady said. "Which'll be a cool time for them to come. I don't think they have Halloween in Lebanon."

"Man, it's HOT in here, Brady," I said. "It must be over a hundred degrees."

"A hundred and fifty, actually. It pulls the excess moisture out of your body."

"Doesn't that make you lose weight?" I asked.

"Yes, a little," she said.

So I bolted out of there and never did get a chance to bring up my theory. But it shouldn't matter. Expiration date on the relationship is TWO DAYS from now anyway.

irony

Wednesday 9/27

Guess what day it is? Day 34!!! Yay! FINALLY!! I have been so, so patient and calm, (well, calm) and now it will PAY OFF! I wonder what time the break-up will happen? Statistically speaking, it should be at 2:45—which is the time the two of them got off the airplane from Rome that day my life changed—but seeing how it's almost 2:45 right now, and Brady and Giulio aren't even together, it would be hard for them to break up. Ironic, isn't it, that you have to be together in order to break up.

(We reviewed literary terms in class today, which is why I am so up on my irony at the moment. English teachers always seem to find a way to teach about irony, every year, and I always seem to forget what it means within a matter of minutes.)

On second thought, you actually <u>can</u> break up when you're not together, like by phone, or a letter, or, say, text message. Who knows—maybe Brady has already done the deed, and Giulio has a message waiting for him to read after English class. Assuming she's the one doing it, that is. I can't get a read on that, seeing how they get along really, really well, and there's no

83

sign that either might not like each other anymore.

(I think that might be another example of irony. This particular ironicality is, I believe, something called "situational irony," because it happens in situations, I guess.)

If she is the one, I hope Giulio doesn't take it too hard. He's not had the best day. In his bio class, he got his test back—the one I "helped" him study for. And let's just say the letter grade he got on it could start spelling the name of a certain cute girl he knows. (And I don't mean Brady.) I told him I'd try to find him a new tutor.

Our first football game was yesterday afternoon. (Football being in my life may be an example of "cosmic irony," which sounds very cool, but really isn't, since it has a whole lot to do with bad luck, which pretty much defines my football experience.) Everyone kept calling it a scrimmage, but it sure looked like a game to me. The other team came to our school on a bus, they had uniforms on, they played football against us for two hours . . . I don't know much about sports, I realize, but I think that's what happens at a game. Also, just before it started, Coach tossed me the scorebook, and said, "DELIA! FIVE MINUTES TO GAME TIME!"

Because I'm sure my look of fear was classic retro horror movie (eyes open wide, mouth in a large "o"—I think my hands may have been on my cheeks, even), Coach began quickly explaining the scoring system. This is what I heard:

BLAH FIRST DOWN BLAH SECOND DOWN
BLAH BLAH BLAH THIRD DOWN BLAH BLAH
BLAH BLAH BLAH FIELD GOAL BLAH BLODDY
BLAH PENALTY BLAH BLAH TOUCHDOWN
BLIPPITY BLOPPITY TACKLE AND BLAH
BLAH BLAH.

Then he scurried off, screaming at the top of his lungs, "ALL ENDS OVER HERE!"

"How rude," I said to the (usual large group of unusually large) players who were hanging around me. "I really don't think employees of a high school should be calling students 'ends.'"

"He's referring to players who are defensive ends, because I think they're working out the quarterback-rush plays," I heard someone say, and since that didn't sound like the typical response of a person on the team, I looked over and saw that it was Richard.

"There are also tight ends on the offensive line," he went on. "But I don't think Coach is calling them, since we're starting on defense today."

Then the whistle blew, and I think Richard noticed the look of terror on my face, because he started explaining things to me as they were happening.

"Okay, it's first and ten, and yada yada," he began. "Yards rushing, yada, number 86, yada, the blitz is on . . ."

"Blintzes!" I said. "They're yummy with cream cheese."

". . . third and eight, na na na na, sack, na na na na, he's a good receiver . . ."

"Well," I said, "how hard is it to receive, really? It's giving that's tough."

". . . long pass, blah blah blop, touchdown!"

After which there was some cheering, and many of the guys on the field held their arms straight up in the air.

"What horrible pit stains," I commented. "That must be embarrassing for them."

"So, Delia, you mark down six points for the Cougars," Richard said, pointing to the book.

"Is that us?" I asked.

"Uh, no, we're the Titans," he said patiently, but with one of those looks you would give someone who, standing at an ice cream truck, orders a Big Mac.

"Oh, yeah, I knew that," I said.

"I tell you what," Richard said, "I'll enter all the numbers this time, and you can watch."

"Oh, thanks, Richard. I love it when you speak math," I said, my sweetest, most appreciative smile on my face as I handed him the book.

This action made him turn quite pink (a very pretty shade, though—my lip gloss color, actually). "Not much chance I'll be playing any time soon, anyway."

"I don't get why they put, like, twice as many people on the team as they need," I said. Then, tapping his shoulder pad, I added, "But you do look kind of cute in this get-up, Richard."

Then his skin tone changed to something VERY close to magenta (definitely NOT my lip gloss shade), so I figured I better just keep quiet and let him score. He tried to explain the game as he went along, but I couldn't see much of what he was scribbling in there, since I didn't want to scooch too awfully close. And it's not because he smelled of B.O. like the other players—a benefit of not playing is not reeking—it was just because he seems to get so embarrassed when I'm too close that I was afraid he might turn so red he'd burst into flames. Which wouldn't be good. For either of us.

Soon I got to thinking about something other than the game that I was (not) scoring, and I asked him, "Are you good at bio, too?"

"Pretty good, I guess," he said.

"Someone I know needs help," I told him.

"Someone?" he asked with that tone that suggests that YOU might actually be the "someone" you are talking about.

"No, I don't need help," I said. "Or, I mean, I do need help with bio, but I'm kind of BEYOND help."

"So who is it?" he asked.

"Giulio, the Italian exchange student," I said.

"Why doesn't Brady help him? She's probably better than I am at science," he said.

"You know Brady, the super-jock," I said. "She doesn't have a whole lot of time. I don't know why she even decided to have a boyfriend, with how busy she is. I mean, a person needs to pay attention to another person if they're together, you know? They need to make time so they can be close and help each other. You know, be touchy-feely—uh, I don't mean 'touchy' as in TOUCH, or 'feely' as in FEEL. I was talking about emotions and time, and, uh, NEVER MIND." And I shut up before I said something stupid(er).

Richard, as I feared, was probably experiencing record core temps in his body, judging by the new color he was displaying. I vowed to myself to never again speak a word to this poor, kind boy, lest I mar him for life.

Guess what? I'm .5 pound heavier than last weigh-in!! This is great! I feel the power! I've been exercising like an exercising MACHINE. I thought I was getting tumors in my calves, but—according to Brady—there are actual muscles in those parts of the body, and mine are getting big! Wow!

(That may be an example of irony, but I no longer have any recollection of the meaning of that term.)

Lucky 34, HERE I COME!

goals

Today, Delia's poetry blabborama features . . . TERZA RIMA!

This is a poetry form I feel I know a lot about, actually, because I listened so unbelievably, super-duperly, <u>molto-buonoly</u> well today. Why, you might ask? Because much of the instruction came from our TERZA RIMA expert: Giulio, the Italian Renaissance maniac.

Yes, it turns out that this poetry form was popular during that Italian time in history when painters stopped painting with eggs and began painting with oil and glass, or whatever it was they did. And it turns out that Giulio is not only really smart when it comes to the art of that time, he also knows about the poetry.

"It is hard to write terza rima in English," he said when the Colonel suggested we use our journals to create our own, "because there are not so many rhyming words in this language as there are in Italian."

This seemed strange at first, but then I had a brainstorm, which led me to the answer. (Before long, I will be talking about what college I want to attend.) Unfortunately, though, before I got a chance to display this evidence of higher intelligence to the class (translation: Giulio), Shakita piped up and said:

"Is that because so many Italian words end in vowels?"

"Yes, that is it," Giulio told her. "You are very smart."

My foot had an uncontrollable spasm at that moment and shot forward, right into Shakita's, uh, end. Which resulted in a bit of a LOOK from her, which resulted in a bit of an "OOPS!" from me.

Terza rima has only three lines per stanza, and there is a really cool REALLY rhyme structure. The first stanza is ABA, and the second is BCB, and the third is CDC, and the fourth is DED, and on and on for as long as you want. When you feel like stopping, you just end with a single line ending with the middle rhyme of the last stanza.

I'm watching Giulio, and he is very busy writing in his journal. I'm sure he is writing his terza rima in Italian. I wish I could do that. I know! I'll write in English, with a twist of Italian! You know, two languages, like in that <u>Spanglish</u> movie. But this will be Italiglish—

I discovered last night-o
that I have gained ANOTHER half-pound-a!
This is INSANE-o!

I MUST get to the mall-a
to find a new top to show off-io
this grand total of one and a half pounds-a!

I am CERTAIN it will-io
be in all the right places, so I will-ina
hop the Metro to the mall-io

Just as soon as I get out of this class-ina!!

Oh, rats-ia! I just realized that I can't go to the mall today. There's a football game tonight, and the bus is leaving right after school. This, I am told, is our REAL first game. The scrimmage, I have learned, did not count in the team's standings. Which is the win-loss record, according to Richard, who is teaching me SO MUCH about football. Perhaps, if my life with Giulio doesn't work out, I have another option: to become a professional football team manager.

About that life with Giulio . . . day 34 came and went, day 35 came and went, and day 36 has come and is threatening to "went" with no break-up occurring. I do NOT understand it. But I will forge ahead and keep my goals prominently in front of me.

Perhaps that new top I plan to buy will also help "keep my

goals prominently in front of me."

Speaking of tops, I can't believe I'm wearing a big, bulky, hide-everything-you-don't-got football jersey today. I feel ridiculous. The tag in it claims it to be a men's small, but I've seen LOTS of men who are WAY smaller than THIS thing.

I tried to explain to Coach that I could, in no way, wear this shirt today, or any day, really, but he insisted that "EVERY PLAYER MUST WEAR THE TEAM JERSEY TO SCHOOL ON GAME DAY TO INCREASE SCHOOL SPIRIT." (I don't think his voice has any volume control.) And when I pointed out that I'm not, actually, a player, he went off on that COMMITMENT-COMMITMENT-COMMITMENT thing again, so I said, "Thank you, goodbye now," and I left (to go purchase some earplugs).

To make matters worse, the manager's jersey has the number 00 on the front. Very large. In the chest area. As in, "prominently in front of me." But, maybe (hopefully) I am the only one noticing how uber bizarre this looks, because no one has come out and laughed at me, and I haven't noticed any whispering in the halls. Still, this whole jersey fiasco is doing a fairly good job of ruining my day. (That and the day-36 thing.)

I have to say, though, that having the entire football team in jerseys HAS seemed to "increase school spirit," judging by how excited they all are. Although I think they sometimes are forgetting that they don't have the rest of the uniform on (for instance the helmet and body padding) given the level of force of the shoulder-butting and head-butting and butt-slapping that's been going on between them in the halls. I noticed a few of them in the nurse's office with ice packs on various parts of their bodies.

The Colonel doesn't seem to really appreciate all this spirit, since it has involved teenage football players acting more like, uh, Teenage Mutant Ninja Turtles. (Not really, but that insisted on coming out of my brain.) One guy had one of those little water bottles that are shaped like grenades—who in the world thought that was a good product idea, I want to know—and it was going back and forth across the back of the room, with footballers yelling, "GO OUT FOR A PASS" and "DIS DA BOMB!" and "TIGHT THROW, MAN!" and "PUMP IT!" and other spirited phrases like that.

So, water bottles have now gone the way of the chachkas and cell phones. The Colonel has banned them entirely.

Shakita didn't appreciate this new action on his part and said, "How is it fair to punish a whole class for the actions of the few? That sounds like discrimination to me."

The Colonel responded with one of those sighs that seems as if it will suddenly deflate your body and make you flit around the room like a shrinking balloon.

The football dudes have continued to display their team spirit throughout our journaling. They have created a little football with someone's tied-up sock (ew).

Shakita has just flashed one of her note-signs to me. It says:

WHAT, EXACTLY, IS THE GPA REQUIREMENT FOR FOOTBALL? 1? AND WHY DO YOU LET THEM DRESS YOU UP IN THAT SEXIST WAY WITH THOSE TARGETS ON YOUR BOOBS?"

I will now be crawling under my desk. Goodbye.

Tuesday 10/3

We must have really burned the Colonel out last Friday, because we have a sub today. She smells like cigarettes and claims to be a choir teacher. She's subbing, she says, because—how surprising—she's out of work.

It's more crazy in here than it was the other day, too, even though no one is in a football jersey. The flying objects are all paper-based today, of the airplane or spitball (gross) variety.

The football game was interesting on Friday. We took the bus to a school at the other end of the county. The guys continued to act all WACK, and I was stuck on the bus with them for two whole hours because traffic was snarled. And it started raining the minute we left and got harder and harder as we sat on the highway. I figured we were going to get there and be told the game was cancelled and then have to turn around and spend another two hours on the bus getting back to school. But, NOOOOO, we actually played in the pouring rain. People were sitting in the stands with garbage bags over their heads. What is WRONG with sports fans?

I think we lost, but I'm only the scorekeeper. Richard helped me (a.k.a. kept the actual score) again, while I held an umbrella over us. The opposing team's manager gave me the umbrella when we arrived, and I thanked him very enthusiastically for being so considerate of my well-being. Then he told me it was to keep the scorebook dry.

Richard was, again, making a very fine attempt at teaching me the rules of the game. He told me, again, where to put the 6 when a touchdown was made, and where to put the 1 when an extra point was scored by the ball being kicked over the goal posts. And where to put the 3 when the ball also got kicked over the goal posts but in a different situation—which is really confusing, you have to admit—and after a really long time of this (easily five minutes), I asked him: "So what inning are we in now?"

"Football has quarters," Richard told me with a kind look, but one that also might be used when you see a dog rolling along the sidewalk in one of those broken-hip carts. "And we're still in the first quarter."

"The FIRST? How many are there?"

"Four," Richard said. "A 'quarter' means that something is divided into four parts. Like money—four quarters equal one dollar."

"This is why I love math," I said. "It makes so much sense."

He went on to show me how you have to keep track of the number of yards a player runs, and when he got to talking about averages, I realized he might be a good person to ask a question that had been on my mind.

"Uh, Richard, " I said. "What is an average REALLY all about, anyway?"

"It's basically the mean," he said. "When you have several quantities, you add all those together and then divide by the number of quantities, and that's the average."

"Yeah, all that, but what if something is supposed to happen in, like, 34 days, and it still hasn't happened in, like, 36 days? What is that about?"

"It's just that if the thing you're talking about happens more than once, then it could happen one time in 40 days, and another time in 28 days, and that would still average 34."

"So, what you're telling me is that if something is supposed to happen in 34 days, on average, then it could happen any other time at all, and may NEVER happen in 34 days?"

He nodded.

"This is why I hate math," I said. "It makes no sense."

Richard laughed at me then, but in a sweet, football-mentor-ish way.

The guys were very subdued the whole way back. It's amazing

the effect losing has on testosterone levels. A few of them even got to talking to me about Halloween. It seems that a small group of footballers (four, to be exact) have been planning their Halloween costumes. This surprised me, actually. I didn't figure any of these guys to be into dressing up.

"I'm Wolverine," one guy said, very matter-of-factly, and then started pointing around at the others, adding, also very matter-of-factly, "he's Magneto, he's Cyclops, and he's Professor X."

So I responded by saying, very matter-of-factly, "Huh?"

"We're X-Men," Wolverine said.

"The comic book <u>X-Men</u>, not the TV <u>X-Men</u>," Magneto added.

"I'm so glad you cleared that up," I said in a relieved sort of way (though I don't have a clue what the diff is).

"We're making the costumes ourselves," Cyclops said. "The biggest challenge for me is the sun visor, from a design standpoint. It has to be incorporated into the overall hood and body suit."

"I wish that were the extent of MY challenges," Professor X said.

"Uh, no offense meant or anything," I piped in, "but aren't the X-Men kind of . . . how do I say this . . . silly?"

"Actually, X-Men are very serious," Wolverine said.

"I am a Holocaust survivor, fighting for human rights causes," Magneto said.

"And I fight racism," Professor X said. "Which is how I became a paraplegic."

"Wow. Sorry about all that," I told them. "So, uh, why are we having this conversation?"

"We need someone to be Rogue," Wolverine (who is apparently the spokesperson for these X-Men) explained.

"Uh, Wolfie," I said, "have you noticed that I'm not, exactly, a 'Man' sort of person?"

"Rogue is a female X-Man," he said.

"We're planning a costume work session for Sunday," Cyclops said, looking at me very hopefully.

Magneto snapped his fingers then and said, "I forgot, I have to study for a physics test on Sunday. But I'll get there."

"I'll be a little late, too," Prof X said. "I have youth group. But I really need to work out what to do about a wheelchair."

Then they went on to entice me by describing the outfit they've been designing for this Rogue character (as in, me), which includes—according to some of them—yellow and green striped leggings and platform boots.

I caught the eye of one of our burliest, meanest-on-the-field ends or backers or liners or whatevers, and I did that heads-down, side-to-side look-thing to get across the question "Are these guys for real?"

He smiled like a five-year-old (missing teeth, and all) and said, "Second stringers, for two years running. They're cool."

"Personally," Wolfie was saying, "my vote was to not make Rogue look like the action figure, but to have that sleek gown with the criss-cross bodice from her first appearance."

Feeling as if I had stepped into a Marvel Comics edition of Project Runway, I stared at them, open-mouthed, while they discussed various issues surrounding the Rogue costume. This was NOT what I had expected from guys of the large, football variety, so I was struck speechless. That is, until Magneto said:

"All right, the cape may be optional, but the dyed hair is a must-do."

"Time out!" I cried. "I'm not dyeing my hair."

"It's just a shock of white in the front," Prof X said. "You'll look terrific."

"No, I won't look terrific," I said, "because I won't be DOING that."

"Well, we could use washable white hair paint," Wolfie said. "It's not the effect I was going for, but if that's a deal breaker for you, we'll compromise. Okay?"

I nodded, which I believe they must have taken as my agreement to be the Rogue, because it was followed by a lot of high-fiving.

(It's amazing what a simple NOD can get a person into. I'm thinking of investing in a neck brace to stay out of trouble.)

"So, what do we do in these costumes?" I asked. "I haven't trick-or-treated in a few years."

"Things like costume parties," Wolfie said.

"There's a Seventies costume party on Halloween at the community center near Nate's house," Cyclops added.

"Who's Nate?" I asked.

"Me," Magneto said.

"Oh! You have real names!" I said, trying to make a little joke, but they all looked at me like I was a crazy person (and not a normal, comic book character like the rest of them).

"Finally, we have our missing Rogue!" Cyclops exclaimed randomly, after a few minutes of awkward silence.

"Yeah, with a missing X-Man, you'd be W-Men," I said, attempting, again, to get one, teensy little laugh out of them, but it just produced similar stares.

Which, of course, worried me, considering how important a sense of humor is to my very existence. But I did not give up hope! I figured their senses of humor just needed to be revealed, and I would surely see this on Sunday when I spent all that costume-related quality time with them. After all, I asked myself, how could four football players who dress up as superheroes NOT have a sense of humor?

The answer to that question—I found after the costume work session—is: VERY EASILY. Nice guys, but they take their X-stuff WAY too seriously. Even when Wolfie took a group picture of us, they did several retakes to make sure no one was smiling.

(That pic is now on FaceBook, apparently with me tagged. I figured this out when about a dozen different people I don't know said, "Hey, Rogue!" when they passed me in the halls today.)

I did manage to squeeze in a shopping trip to look for a new top this weekend, though. Went to a mall that's about twenty minutes away if you drive, but we (Brady and I) had to take a long bus ride (it's a big weekend for long bus rides), since not one relation of ours was willing to take us there. They all said they had to clean our houses, or shop for our food, or cook our meals, or work to make money so we could buy things, so they didn't have time. (And teenagers are called selfish. Sheesh.) But none of that has anything to do with anything, except to avoid the subject at hand, which is:

The 1.5 pounds I gained and all the exercises I did have resulted in me needing a bigger clothing size, yes, but not the exact sort of clothing I had in mind. What I need is bigger jeans. My top size is the same. I didn't want to believe that I'd experienced a no-growth situation (at least in the target zone), so I went to the bra department, to see if maybe cup-size would be more sensitive to the changes that I had been working on. But, NOOOO, my cup size is still the same. (Now, if I could just switch that size for my interim grade in band, I'd have a 4.0 in the class, and my bazooma would be, uh, in C-major . . . so to speak.)

Since I had not explained to Brady the precise nature of my exercise goal, I kept my displeasure to myself until I was alone in a dressing room. Then I looked in the mirror and did one of those maniac yelling things. Only silently, like a mime. Which got some positive energy going for some reason and turned out to be (you might say, given the next idea I had) very UPLIFTING.

"Brady," I called to the next dressing room, where she, too, was trying on bras (though with much better results, I'm sure). "I've got an idea. I'm getting one of those instant-bosom type bras."

"What, do you add water?" she asked.

"Oh, very funny," I said. "I'm talking about the shapely, wonder-bra jobbie I saw out there. What do you think of that?"

"I don't know what you're talking about," she said.

"You wouldn't, would you?" I said. "It's one of those very SHAPELY bras—comes with curves, you know?'

I expected her to tell me that I should appreciate the way I am, and that it's not all that fun having big boobs, and how they get in the way when you're running, and all that kind of stuff. But you know what she said?

"Go for it."

Which (a bit miffed) I did. I'm wearing it now. It feels as if my chest is encased in foam. Which it is, I guess. I may look like Barbie. In body armor.

A paper wad has just hit me in the chest, and it bounced almost to the ceiling.

Memo to self: Don't play Ping-Pong with this thing on.

potential

Thursday 10/5

Before class started today, Giulio stopped me at the door and said, "Delia, I want to give you something to see." Which made me quite excited, as you might imagine, and got me thinking that maybe my new, uh, Wonder-Woman-ish bra came with some super powers in addition to its super-other-ness. Especially since Giulio's "something" turned out to be jewelry.

"I made this with glass beads I bought in Venice," he said. "And this bead here," he said, lifting with his index finger a very dark blue star with shimmering speckles, "I bought on the island of Murano."

"It's beautiful," I said, feeling very cosmic all of a sudden and taking the bracelet out of Giulio's soft, artistic hand. It was made with elastic thread, and I slipped it onto my wrist, easily. "I love it," I said. (Squeaked, actually.)

It was amazing there, sparkling in the classroom's fluorescent light. The perfect way to celebrate a triumphant DAY 42, since this was OBVIOUSLY shaping up as the BIG BREAK-UP DAY. Forty-two, I decided that moment, would be my FAVORITE number FOREVER, and I started having dreamish thoughts about the number . . . it could be the number of people at our wedding, and the number of the house we buy in Italy, and maybe Giulio's soccer shirt number as he strolls up to the door, with me inside with 42 children—AAAAH! (Sorry, freaked myself out for a sec.)

"Brady says blue is her favorite color," Giulio said. "Do you think she will like to wear it?"

"Oh, I'm sure," I said. "I can share with my best friend."

He gave me a curious expression at that moment. One that you might give a cat that you find lounging on your sofa, smoking a cigar. "Maybe I am not using my English well. This is for Brady."

So I handed it back to him and sort of laughed in a very unattractive, snortish way, and I said I knew that, and I was just KIDDING, and yes, yes, of course Brady would love it, and etc. But what I was thinking was: I HATE 42, I will NEVER say that number AGAIN, I will SKIP it when I'm counting. I will never BE 42 . . .

"I am hoping it will be a good luck charm for her hitting at baseball games," he said.

"That's very thoughtful, Giulio," I said. (But I was still thinking: I HATE 42, that is the WORST number in the, uh, number thing—it's UGLY, it SMELLS . . .)

Shakita appeared at that moment and interrupted my 42-bashing by saying, "Homecoming float planning today. Slide by before you go for your daily dose of sado-masochism."

"Translated, that means?" I said, but not to her, since she had swept by and was already at her desk.

"She means that her club is making a large display for the homecoming parade, and she wants you to help plan it before you go to football practice," Giulio said.

"How do you know all that?" I asked him. "You're from a whole different country."

"Homecoming has been on the morning announcements," he said. "It is a week from Saturday, and it involves the first home football game and a parade and a semi-formal dance in the night."

"Giulio, I know what!" I said. "You should help with this float thing. You're an artist."

"But you know I cannot join this 'Gender Neutral' club that you and Shakita are doing together," he said.

Wincing at how weird that sounded, I replied, "Well, Giulio, uh, I've, been, um, wanting to explain some things to you about that club. It's, uh . . ."

And I didn't know how to finish that, seeing as I haven't yet been to a meeting, and I don't really KNOW what it is.

"I understand those things, Delia," Giulio said. "You don't need to feel uncomfortable. We are very open-minded in Italy, and I am not judging. It is just a matter of my personal orientation toward life."

My mouth started making sounds like, "Bah, wuh, ah, na," while the words inside my brain were much clearer, but more along these lines: "This is ALL YOUR FAULT, 42. You call yourself a NUMBER? YOU'RE not a number, YOU'RE a MOUSE!"

Luckily, the bell saved me from further ridiculousness going on inside and outside my head, and I went to my desk and sat down.

Today's poetry theme was "The American Women's Movement." The Colonel was very excited about the poems from the period, and he and Shakita were getting along very well, for once. They both agreed that these writers had a great influence on history and that the peaceful nature of the change proved that "the pen is mightier than the sword." Apparently, the movement started in the 1960s with a desire to change the "desperate position of housewives" and ended in the 1970s with some "bra burning." Which I think might not be a bad idea for today. At least for purposes of this particular bra I'm wearing. Besides being highly uncomfortable, I'm blaming it for some extra, unwanted attention I've been getting suddenly.

All during class today, notes were appearing on my desk, relayed up the row of desks behind me. They were from the tight ends, or defensive ends, or whatever other ends populate the back end of this classroom. And whenever the Colonel turned to write on the white board, some of them held up little signs in my direction, too. It seems they were trying to out-note each other, in pursuit of one thing:

They want to take me to the homecoming dance.

Sure, it might not be the bra that is attracting them. It might be a charming personality. Or it could be my job as the team manager that has caught their attention. They may think I can help with their football careers, what with my IN with Coach and everything.

Okay, it's the bra. Perhaps the best thing to do is destroy the thing before it develops its own personality.

In the olden days of my life, I would have been pretty excited about all this attention, and I would have made myself a neat little list of all the guy's names, and I would have thought through the pros and cons of each of these possible date choices, and I would have—maybe at the very last minute, just to mix things up a little—picked the PERFECT one.

But today I am just finding this very annoying. I mean, the whole class (translation: Giulio) is seeing this go on, and what if this whole class (translation: Giulio) actually thinks I might go out with a guy like, say, the one who held up the note that read: U + ME = HOMCOMIG.

111

Actually, not all the notes and signs were from the, eh, gray-matter-challenged sorts. Some footballers have brains, of course. My X-Men costume buddies, for instance, are also vying for my attention, and they were even getting a bit clever with their notes. Example: DELIA—<u>MANAGING</u> TO STEAL MY HEART. And here's one that incorporated some poetry: AT HOMECOMING, TO BE IN VOGUE, I WANT TO DANCE WITH FASHIONISTA ROGUE.

Maybe I should just go to the dance with someone. I mean, thanks to the truth about AVERAGES, it's really unlikely Giulio will be available before homecoming. And you know? Some of these guys ARE kind of cute.

Okay, then! I've talked myself into it!

Another note is on my desk. This one, though, is from Shakita. I wonder if she's asking me to the dance . . .

No, she's just bugging me about the float thing. So I wrote back: WHY DO YOU CARE ABOUT THE HOMECOMING PARADE IF IT'S ALL ABOUT FOOTBALL?

Zher answer: WE CAN SPREAD GNA AWARENESS AT THE PARADE.

Took me a sec, but it has sunk in that the Gender Neutral Alliance now has initials. So I wrote back: I'LL THINK ABOUT IT. BUT WHO DO YOU THINK I SHOULD GO TO THE DANCE WITH?

Zhe wrote: I VOTE FOR NATE. HE'S COOL. JOINED GNA, ACTUALLY.

Me: YOU'RE KIDDING.

Shakita: NO, I'M NOT. HE SAYS HE'S GOING TO ASK SOME FRIENDS TO JOIN, TOO. SOMETHING ABOUT WEARING COSTUMES ON THE FLOAT.

Mental note: Avoid all contact with the X-Men between now and homecoming.

That means, of course, that my list of potential date choices has shrunk somewhat. Along with the average IQ. Which may be hovering at about 42.

Yesterday, Brady suggested a "walking tour of the mall"
to celebrate Columbus Day. The two of us were having
breakfast at IHOP when she got this idea, so I responded, quite
enthusiastically: "Yes! We'll get our homecoming dresses!"

"Uh, Deel," she said, "I'm talking about the, uh, MALL—
the reflecting pool, Washington Monument, Jefferson Memorial,
those grassy fields in front of the Smithsonian museums?"

"Yes, of course, right you are," I said, laughing robustly.
"But who was it that thought up the idea of calling that place a
'mall'? I mean, there's NO shopping anywhere. Except maybe
those guys selling watches on the street corners."

"The word 'mall' just means a public walking area," Brady
said.

"Okay, then, very interesting." I said. "So how about this for
an idea: We go do a quickie thing at that mall—like see the
Columbus Memorial, say, to celebrate this holiday —and then
we hop the Metro to the REAL mall!"

"First, there IS no Columbus Memorial on the Mall," Brady
said. "And second, I have no money, and I'm planning to just

find something in my closet that'll work for the dance."

"Well, Brady, I don't know for sure, having never been to a homecoming dance, but I'm thinking that 'semi-formal attire' doesn't usually include clothing with numbers across the chest," I said (quite cleverly, in my opinion).

"Har-har," she said (not very cleverly, in my opinion). "But I'm kind of sick of shopping, anyway."

(Can you believe her level of apathy?)

And then she also added (as if this were what we were talking about), "Speaking of numbers, I've been asking my coach if I can change my jersey number. I'm hoping that will help me get just one hit this season."

"So, no improvement in the baseball department, huh? I'm sorry I haven't had time to get to your games lately, but I've been very busy with my own very demanding sport," I said. And then, after a pause, I added, "Did those words really come from ME?"

"I definitely need a new number," she said. "My batting average stinks."

"Don't talk about averages. I hate averages," I said.

Ignoring that (while, understandably, giving me an odd look), she said, "I'm thinking of 42. Is that too big a number?"

"Don't talk about 42. I hate 42," I said.

This made her give me an even odder look, since, of course,

that had to have sounded pretty random to someone who hasn't actually been in my head lately.

Looking to change the subject, I rubbed the large purplish-green bruise on my arm and said, "A dress with sleeves might be best for me."

"Ow. What happened there?" she asked.

"A tight end fell on me," I said.

"What, are they falling out of the sky?"

"Funny, " I responded (laughing at the visual on that). "One of our players—a tight end, to be more descriptive—got the idea to start head-butting his best friend, but the guy moved just as he was in mid-butt. So he landed on my arm."

"What an idiot," she said. "Who was it, anyway?"

"Adrian. My date for homecoming."

This made her laugh a little longer than need be. Especially considering SHE had helped me with the selection.

(Fuzzy, foggy, dreamy recollection sequence coming up . . .)

It was Friday night, and I had been getting ready for our all-night, girls-only movie and chocolate-a-thon featuring our 17th viewing (but who's counting?) of our latest #1 favorite movie, Wayne's World, when Brady appeared at my door with a football helmet in her arms.

"What are we doing with that?" I asked.

"We're writing the names of each of your football player admirers on a slip of paper, then dropping them in the helmet, then setting the mood for a selection moment, then picking a name out of the helmet," she said, very normally (as if that particular thing had been done on Planet Earth before).

"I had been thinking we might discuss the merits of each candidate," I said. Which got her laughing and basically kept her laughing while we made a pot of chocolate fondue, created a large mound of mouth-sized cubes of angel food cake, and began pigging out on the couch in my basement.

In order to refill our trough and get more fizzy water and do whatever else we needed to do, we paused the movie at the usual spot: in the middle of the scene where Garth and Wayne are lying on their backs waiting for the plane to land. We always try to hit the pause button RIGHT when the plane is DIRECTLY over them, when they're in mid-AAAAAHHHH!!! (It's an art to get that just right.)

Later on in the movie, I realized I had forgotten to visit the "little girls' room" during that break, so I told Brady we had to pause it again so I could go upstairs, but she grabbed the remote and said, "Stairway denied!" Which resulted in a bit of a wrestling match that Brady was winning until I spied my trusty Sharpie pen on the floor nearby. I picked it up, took the top off, and began drawing pictures on her leg.

Brady HATES it when I write on her body, so when she realized I was "getting creative," she stopped wrestling me and looked at her calf. It was quite cutely decorated with an alien head.

"You think you're funny, I guess," she said.

"Yes, I am the Wayne Campbell of our little pair," I said.

"No, I don't think so," Brady said. "I am Wayne."

"Uh, whose basement are we in when watching this movie?" I asked.

"Yours, but that's just because my house doesn't have a basement," she said.

"Exactly my point," I said. "And who is the cuter of the two of us—the Robo-babe, the Babe-raham Lincoln—as opposed to the brainier, weird-looking one. Huh?"

"Are you suggesting that I am like Garth?" Brady asked.

"Yes, I am," I said. "And I think you're even starting to look a little like him, you know, the way people start to look like their dogs?"

This resulted in another Brady lunge, but I held up my Sharpie, which made her instantly calm down.

(I guess the Colonel is right! The pen IS mightier than the sword!)

And even though I would reach over occasionally and pat Brady on the head and say, "That's a good little Garthy," she remained on the couch until the end of the movie—or all three endings, actually. After the last one (the "Mega-Happy Ending"), she leaped up and said:

"It's . . . the SELECTION MOMENT! And for the right mood, we'll need an aromatherapy candle."

"For the guys in that helmet, we'll need something WAY stronger than that," I said.

"So why are you considering any of them?" she asked.

"Some are cute," I said. "In a football sort of way. And, anyway, my best date—VU—is not available."

"Who?" she asked.

"Vu," I repeated.

"What does that mean?"

"Doesn't it mean 'you' in Italian?"

"No, I think that's 'tu.'"

"Okay, whatever. Now I've forgotten the point I was making."

"You wished you could go with me to the dance," Brady said. "And I kind of feel the same way, actually."

"You want to go to the dance with you, too? Or, tu, too?" I asked, trying to be funny, in order to cover up my sudden enthusiasm over this unexpected comment.

"We just aren't hanging out as much lately, you know?" she said.

"But you do want to go with Giulio, right?" I asked Brady, while my brain tried to channel to her: SAY NO, SAY NO, SAY NO.

"Oh, yeah," she said. "It's just that I've been wondering lately if maybe, you know, Giulio is kind of, uh, the reason I'm not getting any hits this season."

"Oh, like having a boyfriend is sort of a Superman-and-Kryptonite thing and sucks the energy out of you. Or like a LEECH, or maybe a VAMPIRE. Right?"

"Uh, no. I'm just wondering if Giulio being at games is giving me the bad luck. I don't know how to tell him, but I wish he'd skip going to just one game, so I can see."

"When's the next one?" I asked.

"Wednesday night."

"Well, okaaay," I said. "It'll be a burden, Brady, but I'll distract your gorgeous, Italian dream machine for the eve. Consider it done, and may the night be a big hit for you."

"Very punny, and thanks, Delia," she said. "One thing, though: BEHAVE."

"Don't WORRY," I said. "No matter what random thoughts might enter my mind on matters of Euro-hotties you drag home

with you from Mediterranean cruises and then immediately
keep for yourself, I wouldn't act equally greedy and try to steal
him or anything."

"Okay, then," she said. "Let's get the homecoming helmet
and see who's date-worthy for you."

That's when I picked Adrian. And I told him the news at
Saturday morning practice. Which, looking back, probably
prompted the whole head-butting incident—obviously a happy,
triumphant gesture. Until it went wrong. On my arm.

So—to make a short story really, really, really long—I
bowed out of the "walking tour of the Mall," claiming I needed
to spend the afternoon on my couch, icing up my football
injury. Which I did, for five minutes, until I was successful at
convincing my mother to take me dress shopping.

I found an excellent little black number. It has sleeves,
which is good, but the dress doesn't quite work with the shape-
shifter bra—something I'm glad to report. I am SO retiring that
thing. I would soon be needing a guy-swatter.

denial   Thursday 10/12

Yay! The homecoming game is this weekend! I am PUMPED!
(Did I just use the word "pumped"? Scary.)

Oh, man, though, we have had INJURIES lately. These guys
have been so excited about this weekend that they can't stop
DESTROYING each other.

There was the weight-room injury, which occurred when
one of those doughnut-looking weights slipped off the end of a
bar and landed on a fullback's toe. (Ouch.) And the locker-room
injury, which involved a locker door being fully closed on a
linebacker's arm. In regard to that particular injury, I've been
wondering if someone else accidentally caused this, or if the
linebacker somehow managed to close the door on his own arm
(which would be a very sad thing). But I may never know, since
I was not a witness to that, since I can't go in the guys' locker
room, for the obvious reason—I don't own a gas mask.

Some injuries even occurred on the field during practice,
like the one where our varsity quarterback threw a pass to the
wide receiver, who tripped over the junior varsity defensive
tackle and flew into the end zone so hard that he hit the goal

post and dislocated his shoulder. (Am I sounding like a sports announcer now, or WHAT?)

But things are going quite well with the GNA float. At least according to Shakita. And Wolfie. And the other X-Guys. I've stayed away from helping with that, using up just about every excuse I've got—headache, in-grown toenail, PMS (that one worked the quickest to get the guys to leave me alone)—so I don't somehow get roped into being on that float, dressed in green and yellow boots for the entire school body (translation: Giulio) to see. Hopefully they are done by now, since there was a special work session last night. When Magneto asked if I could help, I told him that Brady had an important game. He told me to wish her luck, but I said, "Maybe you should just text her. I'm not actually going." He looked at me weird and started to say something, but I handed him Brady's number and fled.

I told Giulio I was taking him out for cake to celebrate his birthday.

"But my birthday is not until April," he told me as we were walking into town.

"Well, it's a custom in America to start celebrating birthdays ahead of time," I said. "Ideally, a whole YEAR ahead of time."

"I like you, Delia. You are a very funny person," he said.

Which made me start having the entirely wrong thoughts

about this little evening with Giulio, but I snapped back to reality when my phone rang its text-message ring. It was Brady.

—uh, deel? who is magneto?

—my x-friend

—ur not friends n e more?

—no. I mean yes. I mean no. he's one of those x-men guys.

—y did he text me to wish me luck?

—he's nice. a holocaust survivor.

—how is that possible?

—IDK

—okaaaay. how's giulio?

—he's fine, yes, fine, good. he says hi and good luck.

—uh-oh. that might have just given me bad luck. bye

Last night, as it turns out, was a very active text-messaging night, which was probably good, since the interruptions kept my mind from getting too carried away in the Giulio-and-me department. The next text conversation was with Wolfie, who was complaining to me that (a) I wasn't there and they really needed to do some "fittings," and (b) Shakita was making them refer to themselves as "Z-Men" while they were on the float, and (c) they couldn't possibly call themselves that, since they were X-Men and "a denial of such would go against core principles."

Then Shakita texted me for a while, and that went like this:

—these guys r not serious enuf

—actually they r the most serious people I've ever met

—they act like the float is just about people parading around in costumes

—isn't it?

—where r u? we need ur help

—bye! battery is going!

(Well, it was going sometime.)

Prof X texted to complain that the float wasn't handicapped accessible, and then Wolfie texted again to ask if I preferred green armbands or silver, and then Shakita texted to ask why my battery was still working, and then Brady texted at the end of her game to say:

—STRUCK OUT ALL NIGHT

I have just been jolted back to my immediate life by the Colonel's approaching footsteps. I have to look Englishy!

Okay, he's gone now. He did that proud head-nodding thing again, even though I am so caught up in this story of my own personal life that I don't even REMEMBER what he suggested we might do in our journals today. I think it had something to do with song lyrics. Maybe he thinks my text message conversations are songs.

Oh, why not?

Brady and I went to the parade, and it was actually pretty fun. The GNA float was a pickup truck decorated mostly with large cardboard words—ZHE, ZHER, etc. The Zs are what really stuck out, so it looked like a club about sleeping. Which would be a very popular idea for a club, I think, since that activity is definitely big with high school students, particularly in class.

When the float rolled by the spot where we were standing, my X-Men—er, Z-Men—buddies yelled, "KIDNAP!!" and jumped off the thing and swooped me up and put me in the back of the truck. I managed to escape pretty quickly, but not without almost getting knocked out by a large Z that fell off the side and hit me in the head.

If I HAD been knocked unconscious, I might have actually spent the evening with my homecoming date, since Adrian broke his nose during the game and went to the hospital. Luckily, I had selected a runner-up from the helmet that night with Brady. It was the quarterback, Dante. But unluckily (for him), he, too, was wheeled off the field. A broken limb or some such thing . . . I can't keep track of all these injuries. As he was being rolled off into his parents' car, he asked me if he could have a raincheck for next homecoming.

"I may be living in Italy then, sorry," I said, doing my best to give him a concerned and apologetic look.

"Is that a different school district?" he asked just as the car door was shutting (thankfully).

"You know," I said to Richard after that, while we were working on the scorebook (okay, he was), "it's amazing how many players we've lost this season. What a VERY dangerous game this is!"

"I guess you've figured out why the team is so big," he said.

Then (cue the staff), Coach appeared, and said, "RICHARD, YOU'RE IN!"

"No!" I cried. "You can't go, Richard!"

Picking up his helmet from the ground and pushing it onto his head, he said, "That's really nice of you, Delia. But I'll be okay."

I was actually reacting to his abandonment of the score-book, but I decided not to correct his idea on that. And since I felt bad for my thoughtless, uh, thoughts, I said:

"Richard, if you make it through this, will you be my date for the dance tonight?"

It was a movie-perfect moment—he stood there, turning Technicolor purple, wobbling a bit. I started to wave the EMS team over, but then he gave me a thumbs-up, handed me the scorebook, and jogged onto the field.

I did my best to score. I was really trying to keep up with all the rushing and punting and blitzing and intercepting and pass completions and pass incompletions, and touchdowns and touchbacks and field goals . . . I was a scoring maniac! At the end, I had calculated that we won the game 496 to 2!

Which, of course, wasn't RIGHT, but we did WIN, which I figured out from all the excitement going on at the end of the game. The players suddenly began jumping on top of each other and throwing helmets in the air. It was quite violent, and I thought Richard was hurt in the commotion, because a bunch of guys carried him off the field on their shoulders. But then Coach yelled:

"GO EASY ON THAT BOY!! HE'S OUR SECRET WEAPON!"

Deer-Richard had apparently won the game for us, which meant he and I were WAY POPULAR at the dance, let me tell you. The star quarterback and manager of the WINNING TEAM—oh, yeah, WE were COOL. Peeps were high-fivin' us up and down. It was sooooo strange.

Richard's not a klutz on the dance floor, either, which shouldn't surprise me at this point, I guess, but I still find it hard not to see that uncoordinated elementary school kid when I look at him. But what was really a shocker was how so many girls were all flirtsy-like when they were around him. Which bothered me, since I don't remember them looking at him like that before the big win. I, on the other hand, asked him to be my date to the dance before he became a "secret weapon," showing very clearly my deepness of, uh, depth. So I just did that eyebrow-up-and-a-nod thing to all those girls and made sure Richard and I were engaged in lively conversation whenever they hovered.

Meanwhile, Brady and Giulio were dancing rather closely for a time, and then they just seemed to disappear. That's the first time I've seen them go off alone like THAT, and I haven't talked to either of them since then. Giulio isn't in school today for some reason. And I've been avoiding Brady, because I'm afraid to hear any details about the, uh, seriousness level. I've been unusually busy anyway. Yesterday I volunteered at the Walk for the Homeless, which was (get this) a community service thing (I amaze myself daily) that GNA was doing, and it turned out to be, like, 10 KILOMETERS, which I think is 40 miles, at least. So I slept for the next 15 hours solid.

Well, I don't know how to say this.

Maybe—for reasons I can't begin to comprehend—it would be easier to express what's on my mind if I were to reach back a ways and get into e.e. cummings mode . . .

Br
ady
ha
s bro
ken u
p wi
th Gi
uli
o.

My head should be occasionally pounding into the ceiling with the high spirits and overwhelming delight I should be experiencing, but . . .

I feel bad. I mean, Brady is upset. (I think it's more about the fact that she's still striking out than the actual breakup, but whatever.) And Giulio is upset. BEYOND upset. He's so blue he's INDIGO, man. It's so pathetic that I can't possibly do a thing that would be considered a move on my part. I'll have to wait until he's WAY more over this. Anyway, given that I'm very busy acting as the consoler of both of these people, I have very little time to envision my Italian future at the moment.

Brady says she really likes Giulio but just wants to keep it as friends, because the whole thing has broken her concentration on other "important" stuff.

"My baseball record is totally shot, as you know, and I haven't popped my PR once this cross-country season."

I nodded and tried to look really understanding, hoping she might not catch on that I did not know what "popped my PR" meant.

"It means breaking my personal record," she said, obviously having a reading-Delia's-mind moment.

(I then concentrated hard on NOT thinking about the details of my dream-life with Giulio.)

"And," she went on, "all my grades are low so far this quarter, so I need to concentrate on bringing those up," she said.

"How low?" I asked.

"An A minus in EVERY class," she said.

Thinking this to be a joke, I laughed quite loudly, but stopped abruptly when I remembered I was talking to the person who decided at age five that she would be the valedictorian of her high school class.

(Life is just so much simpler when you shoot for the middle.)

Turns out she had been trying—the night of homecoming when they disappeared—to talk Giulio into this just-being-friends thing, but he can't seem to handle that. Yesterday he was telling me how he can't face her, and it hurts too much, and he might go back to Italy, and other really pathetic stuff. He left school halfway through the day today, because he said he wanted to go home and sleep. He's a wreck. (A cute wreck, though.)

I was explaining all this to Richard after practice yesterday— the current situation with Brady and Giulio, and the resulting stresses on my general life, but without the details of my actual future life with Giulio, of course—and it was one of those things where you expect to look over at the guy next to you and he's turned into a skeleton from all the talking. But Richard actually seemed into it. When I got to the part about how Brady doesn't really have a cheering section anymore, and she's striking out all the time, and there's NOTHING she can do to stop it, he said, "I'd like to go to a game. Want to?"

Not at all sure if this were a date-type question, and definitely not wanting to be in ANY date-type situation, what with Giulio on the loose now, I used a delaying tactic and said I'd get the schedule to him later.

I actually listened to morning announcements today, and guess what I learned? Shakita was just elected president of the Math Honor Society! (What a joiner she is!) This may be good news for me, because I'm in deep trouble with Coach this week, since the scoring of the homecoming game was, uh, a little too, uh, CREATIVE for his taste. And Richard is practicing all the time, so I can't get any help from him these days. I'll write a note to her and see what she thinks of my idea . . .

Okay, this is how our note-conversation just went:

ME: HEY SHAK—HEARD YOU'RE THE MATH WIZ. CAN YOU TEACH ME HOW TO SCORE A FOOTBALL GAME?

ZHER: WHY WOULD I KNOW HOW TO SCORE A FOOTBALL GAME?

ME: THERE ARE INSTRUCTIONS ON THE INSIDE COVER, AND YOU JUST NEED TO READ THEM.

ZHER: WHY DON'T YOU READ THEM, THEN?

ME: HA-HA-HA! YOU ARE SO FUNNY! SO CAN YOU?

ZHER: I GUESS. WHEN?

ME: THERE'S A SCRIMMAGE THIS AFTERNOON.

ZHER: WELL, OKAY.

ME: THANKS! HOW CAN I REPAY YOU?

ZHER: VEEP POSITION AT GNA IS STILL OPEN. HEY, CAN
YOU BELIEVE WHAT THIS INSANIAC WAS TALKING
TODAY? THIS "ADVERTISING AS POETRY" IS SO, SO
BOGUS. IS HE JOKING THAT WE'RE SUPPOSED TO GO
HOME AND FIND ADS IN MAGAZINES AND ON TV THAT
"UTILIZE POETIC DEVICES?" WHO WANTS TO BE DOING
SOMETHING STUPID LIKE THAT?

ME: READ ZINES AND WATCH THE TUBE FOR HOMEWORK?
YEAH, SOUNDS AWFUL.

ZHER: BELL'S ABOUT TO RING. SEE YOU IN ROOM E-11.

ME: FOR WHAT?

ZHER: THE INDUCTION CEREMONY IS TODAY. IT'LL ONLY
TAKE A FEW MINUTES.

Oh, the things I do for football.

I have a big problem. Shakita won't go to the game with me today.

"I told you, you'll do fine," zhe said when I'd asked her for the fifth time. "I can't go to those games. I'd kill the coach if I had to spend five more minutes with him, and then I'd spend the rest of my life in jail."

I think I feel a flashback coming on . . . yes . . . it's Wednesday, and Shakita and I are arriving at the football field for the scrimmage . . .

"HURRY UP, HURRY UP! IT'S ALMOST KICK-OFF!" Coach yelled as we scurried to the bench.

Or, I scurried to the bench. Shakita, she MOSIED. Then she sat down and plopped her school bag onto the seat next to her. This thing is slathered with bumper stickers, which say things like: WOMEN ARE NATURAL LEADERS, YOU'RE FOLLOWING ONE NOW; and I AM THE FUTURE OF AMERICA. BE AFRAID. BE VERY AFRAID; and DON'T MAKE ME RELEASE THE FLYING MONKEYS.

"WHAT DOES THAT MEAN?" Coach asked, pointing to the monkey one.

"It means that you DON'T want me to get mad," she said.

Then, looking at me, Coach said, "WHAT IS SHE ON?"

"I prefer 'zhe,'" Shakita said.

He looked a bit confused, but, seeming to ignore that, he said, "AND WHY IS SHE HERE AT PRACTICE? NO FRIENDS AT PRACTICE."

"Uh, ZHE, please," Shakita sort of sang.

Coach's expression started looking like the Colonel's did that day HE made first contact with Shakita.

"Zhe's here to improve my scoring skills," I said.

"OH, HER NAME IS GEE," he said.

"No, it's Shakita," zhe said.

This made him get all puffed up and (more) irritated, but then someone blew a whistle, which made him dart off in the direction of the football players.

"He responds well to the whistle," Shakita said. "Is he part dog?"

"That would certainly explain some things," I said.

Then Coach barked (hehe) at us that we'd better be ready with the scorebook because the offensive players would be in position in five minutes.

"How rude to call your own players 'offensive,'" zhe said. "What did they do to HIM?"

I explained about the offensive line and the defensive line, and then I showed her the scoring instructions, and—I'm not kidding—she knew how to score by kick-off.

"You go ahead, then, and I'll watch over your shoulder," I said. And then I added (to be extra respectful), "Or do you say 'zoo' instead of 'you'?"

"'You' is already gender neutral," she said, "as in I'll be watching YOU score." And she handed me the pencil and scorebook.

While I was struggling through this very, very mean (but remarkably effective learning) experience, Giulio seemed to appear out of nowhere and sit on the bench with us. He didn't say anything, but just sat, a soccer ball in his lap.

After a very awkward minute or so, I said, "Hi, Giulio."

"Hi," he said. "Has Brady started playing well at baseball now that I'm out of her life?"

"No, actually, she still isn't hitting, Giulio," I said. "So there's that."

He nodded, staring ahead some more, and then said, "Maybe she would have liked me better if I had chosen to play this game of American football."

"But you're morally opposed to it," I reminded him.

"That does not matter anymore," he said.

"Oh, that makes sense," Shakita said. "Throw away your ideals to attract a girl."

"If only I had heard that advice earlier," he said, getting up and wandering off to an open area of the field, where he did some sort of soccer-dribbling drill that involved his feet, knees, head and shoulders, but never his hands. It was mesmerizing to watch this, and not for the usual reason (that being the fact that he is part Roman god).

"He sure can handle a soccer ball, can't he?" I said to Shakita.

"Why don't you just go over and tell that boy that you're hot for him? This is ridiculous," she said.

"How did you know?" I asked her, but she just did that harrumphing sort of thing, and then our attention got diverted by Richard, who was trotting up to us.

"Hey, Delia—you get Brady's baseball schedule yet?" he asked.

"I'll get it to you tomorrow," I told him, and he nodded his, uh, helmet, and then sprinted back to the scrimmage.

"What does Brady HAVE, anyway?" Shakita asked. "Some kind of pheromone, like a honey bee? She's got these guys buzzin'."

"You mean Richard? No, Richard isn't interested in Brady," I said, watching him get in his quarterback position and calling out his HUT-HUT-HUTs to the other players. Then I looked over to where Giulio had been doing that stuff with the soccer ball, but he had obviously given up and was walking away from the fields. I watched as he got smaller in the distance.

And then I had one of those sudden shuddering things, where your whole body goes into seizure-mode for a second.

"What was that?" Shakita asked.

"I don't know," I said. "Just felt all prickly there."

"Probably an acute case of jealousy," zhe said.

"Jealousy?" I repeated.

"Or maybe it's jock itch, but either way you've been around this field too long, Delia."

And that ends today's flashback. Thank you for coming.

Jealousy. She was meaning that I'm jealous of Brady, because Giulio likes her so much, right? Or was she referring to Richard? And, anyway, why do I care? I've got other things to think about, like this tendonitis I'm developing from all the writing I do every other day. Or it could be carpel tunnel syndrome. Luckily, we have a long weekend for teacher work days, which means I won't have to exercise my writing muscles for almost a week.

I feel sad about that, actually, like I'm going to miss you, journal. But I have to close you up, now, and we'll meet again on Thursday and have a chat.

Wait a minute! I'm writing to myself, so I'M the journal. Which means I'm CLOSING MYSELF UP INSIDE IT. HELP! GET ME OUTA—

weird

Many strange things have been happening in the past few days.

STRANGE THING #1

We got our grade updates today, and do you know what I have in English? An A. I think the Earth may explode.

Other space-related news includes . . .

STRANGE THING #2

I had a very bizarre IM conversation yesterday. I rarely IM anymore, since it gets really annoying, and the same people are on there that have been on there for several years (and I'm not kidding about that), and these people act different when they're IMing, like it gives them a personality disorder, or something, so it's always a little uncomfortable when you later run into them in actual person, so you find you are always avoiding them, even though you've known them your whole, entire life. But that has nothing to do with my bizarre IM conversation (except maybe the personality disorder part). Let's see if I can try to recreate it for my journal's enjoyment . . .

KillKirk4591: i am gorkon.

TheRealDeel: i am late for something.

KillKirk4591: i know brady from the ship.

TheRealDeel: the ship? oh! the ship! the cruise!

KillKirk4591: yes. it is there that brady rejected my attempt to be her mate.

TheRealDeel: don't take the brady rejection too personally. she just rejected another guy, too—and he was really good-looking. not that i'm saying ur not good-looking. but if ur not, i'm sure that has nothing to do with y brady rejected u, cuz she would have a reason that's not superficial, u know, like there would have to b some really annoying habit, or the person might be mean, or act weird. so! where r u from?

KillKirk4591: i am from kling.

TheRealDeel: oh, yeah, brady told me u speak klingon. i love listening to foreign languages! r u coming to visit?

KillKirk4591: i will check coordinates.

After that he went on to tell me that there was some issue going on that might interfere with his time. It had something or other to do with Pluto being a dwarf planet, which seemed to trouble him a lot, actually. I tried my best to console him, but I had to go, because it was time for me to experience . . .

STRANGE THING #3

I went to Brady's game this weekend, and—yes, as I promised—I also told Richard about it, so he was there. We were sitting together on the bleachers, and I was going on-and-on-and-on-and-on about how pathetic it's been for Brady, and how we have to be a good cheering section for her, since she swings through every pitch, or hits little bouncers right into the gloves of the infielders who throw her out before she's halfway down the first-base line. (And yes, I know I am sounding all like I know what I'm talking about, but that's just because I now do know what I'm talking about. Sad.) And then, while I was in mid-description about Brady's horrible luck at the plate this season, just to prove me wrong, she HIT A SINGLE. Her FIRST hit of the season.

It became obvious to me, at that moment, that I, Delia, am the power behind Brady's baseball luck. All I have to do is say one thing, and she does the other! I guess this means I will have to go to every game, from now on, to bad-mouth her playing abilities. Oh, the burden of friendship.

Not only did Brady hit a single at that game, she then hit a HOME RUN, then a DOUBLE, then a TRIPLE.

"A triple's the hardest hit in baseball," Richard said. "This is amazing, too, that Brady has had every kind of hit today. She's hit for the cycle. I'm really impressed."

"Yeah, she really sucks big-time," I said.

I wish Giulio had been there, because he would have seen her hitting away, and it would all have become quite obvious that he wasn't her bad luck charm after all. And then maybe he would have stopped being sad.

Turns out he was having a pretty good weekend, though. Since we had the extra days off, he went on a trip with some other exchange students to see an art museum in Philadelphia, which I think is the same place cream cheese comes from. And cheese steaks.

"There is good art there, Delia," he said to me as we were standing outside the door of this class today. "Mondrians, Pollocks, and some excellent sculptures by Alexander Calder, too." He was actually smiling about that, and I was thinking how nice it was for him (and for me, since it's getting me a little closer to feeling comfortable planning my pounce), and then Richard showed up for class.

"I still can't believe those hits Brady had at the game!" he said to me. "I think that might be a league record of some sort." And then he went and sat down.

"Brady was hitting?" Giulio said to me, his smiley face changing to a sad face again.

"Yeah, but it's not you, Giulio, it's me," I said. And I blathered on, trying to explain about my discovery at the game.

"Thank you for trying to make me feel better, but it is clear she has her athletic power back now, and I will never be needed again." And then he went and sat down.

I got off track, there, but here is . . .

STRANGE THING #4

This guy from Texas, AJ, arrived in D.C. this weekend. He's the first of the Mediterranean cruisers to get here. Brady and I met him at a little coffee shop in town, and when we were placing our orders, he said to us, "Mah daddy took me out huntin when ah was tin, an he said, 'Son, you never make a woman pie.'"

"Well, that's pretty similar to what a father might tell a son around here, too," I said. "But without the whole hunting thing, maybe. And usually kids around here just kind of KNOW not to make woman pies without someone telling them."

"His father was telling him never to make a woman PAY," Brady said to me, in the soft, sideways voice you would use to tell someone her fly is down.

"Sorry about that—I'm not so good at understanding Texan," I said to AJ. "The only Texan I've ever heard is George Bush on YOU TUBE, and all I can remember about that is that he says 'nucular.'"

"What's wrong with that?" he asked.

"It's supposed to be nu-clee-ur," I explained.

"Wayll, that's what he said, isn't it? Nucular."

"Um, yeah, that is what he said. So, let's seeee . . . I'll have a tall caramel macchiato."

After we got our drinks and we were sitting in some comfy chairs, chatting, who should walk through the door but Shakita. So we introduced her to AJ, and he said, "What would you like, purdy?"

"I'll get it, but thanks," zhe said, giving him a suspicious look, then drifting over to the counter.

"AJ, it might be a good idea to be a little careful about what types of things you say and, uh, do around here," Brady said to him. "D.C. is sort of different from Texas."

Then—as if to illustrate the point—Shakita plopped her bag down on the table and sat down. AJ was looking over her collection of stickers, and repeated this one: "SEE HILLARY RUN. RUN, HILLARY, RUN."

And then he commented: "Ah could never vote fir a woman as president, because they are jes too emotional."

Which, naturally, caused Shakita to go NUTS on him. And when she was done, she picked up her bag and stormed out of the coffee shop.

We stared after her, kind of stunned, and then AJ said, "Exactly mah point," which made us all crack up, although probably not all for the same reasons.

So, that's the end of strange happenings. Except the strangeness of what we're studying here in class today. I think it's entirely possible that the Colonel made the poetry unit about two weeks too long, because we are SO pushing the outer limits of this thing. Today was "conversation as poetry." We broke into four groups, and at any one time, three groups were having conversations on various topics, and one group was hovering around, listening, and writing the "natural lines of poetry that flow from the spoken word."

"Nothing needs to make sense," the Colonel said before we got started.

"You have to give him points for consistency," Shakita whispered to me.

The topics were (quite logically): feminism, football, and Halloween.

I got to be in the first hovering-listening-writing group, so I fanned out with my paper and pen to capture some of the "natural lines of poetry" that the Colonel was convinced were coming out of my classmates' mouths.

I started at the feminism circle, where Shakita was doing all the talking, as best I could tell. But since she was not actually IN that group and was supposed to be hovering and writing, too, and since the Colonel was heading in the direction of that group at that particular moment to remind Shakita that the hoverer-listeners aren't supposed to talk, I decided to move on to football.

I actually wrote a few lines from the football conversation . . .

A random linebacker said: We are SO going to keep this STREAK GOIN!!!

Adrian, the tight end: After Saturday night, it'll be three in a RIZZLE, dude.

A flirty girl: Want me to write for you, Richard, so you don't strain your throwing arm?

I felt a sudden urge to spew, so I moved on to the Halloween group . . .

CYCLOPS: I finally got the visor to work, so now I'll help you
concentrate on getting that belt right for Rogue.

MAGNETO: So, Rogue, can you please, please stop by for a
fitting. It'll only take five mins—promise! The Halloween
party is Tuesday night, and you haven't tried on the ensemble
since that day we got started. I'm getting nervous that it
won't look good!

ME: I'm getting nervous about that same thing, actually.

The Colonel suddenly appeared at our group at that moment and told me to shut my trap (but he said it in a more teacherly way, of course), which made Shakita loudly point out that she had noticed he was only telling females to be quiet.

"Only females happen to be talking when they're supposed to be listening," he said.

"It's still discrimination," she said.

So he did what most teachers do when backed into a corner: He changed the subject.

"Switch out, everyone," he ordered. "Halloween conversation group start talking about football. Football group start talking about Halloween. Listener-writers change positions with the feminists."

We made it seem much more complicated than it was, because some of my classmates (think: mountain-shouldered types) really didn't understand what he wanted, and the rest of us couldn't resist pretending we didn't understand what he wanted. We were all racing around looking for chairs, like a bunch of six-year-olds at a birthday party. Good times!

But after a few minutes we took pity on the Colonel, who had been getting increasingly frustrated in his attempts to explain the rules, and we sat down in our assigned places, more or less.

"So we're supposed to talk about football?" Magneto said to the Colonel. "I don't really know much about that."

"But you PLAY football," Shakita and I both said at the same time, turning around and staring at him.

"Oh, we just do that for the workout," he said. "To increase strength. For figure skating. We're thinking of giving that a try."

"If we aren't up to the athletic part of it, we can always design the costumes," Cyclops added.

"Then talk about that," the Colonel said, very tiredly.

"It is like Brady and how she runs her cross country, but cares more for her baseball," Giulio said, sadly. I'd hardly noticed him there in our group, since he'd been so quiet and droopy all class.

"So, is that our topic? Baseball?" asked one of the mountain-shoulders who had wandered, confused, into our little circle.

"No, it's feminism," Shakita said.

"Is that like fembots?" another mountain-shoulder asked.

Shakita started to launch into another one of her lectures, so I slapped my hand over her mouth and said to the guy, "Yes."

Shakita—clever girl—managed to get my hand off her mouth without even touching it. She began emitting saliva from her mouth. After about one-half second of that, she was free.

"What," she said, "do those inane 'fembots' have in common with feminism?"

"The first three letters?" I suggested.

There was a bit of laughing from the hoverer-listener-writers that had begun gathering around our conversation, but Shakita quickly shushed them by going off on a rant about negative representations of females in popular movies. They soon left, and we pretty much listened to her until the Colonel decided to give up on the activity altogether and declared it an extra-time-for-journaling day.

My hand will be falling off now. Goodbye.

deal
Monday 10/30

Brady had a game Friday afternoon, and I managed to talk
Coach into letting me skip football practice to go, because I
explained all about how Brady has only had one game where
she's been hitting, and there's this whole superstition thing—
sometimes having to do with socks and hats—and when I got to
the part about her trying different things, including a different
sports bra, he said, "OKAY, OKAY, GO!"

So I high-tailed it to the game and sat there on the bleachers and bad-mouthed her, which wasn't so easy, since I wasn't
WITH anyone and I had to talk to strangers, who gave me some
very nasty looks. Which would have been worth it, but guess
what? It didn't work. She fanned EVERY pitch.

(Did I just say that? Geez. I am SO jock now. I'll need some
kind of exorcism when this is all over.)

Luckily, Tatyana and Noori arrived this weekend, so that
was a distraction that kept Brady from dwelling too much on the
return of her sports failures. We went to the airport to get them
on Sunday, and my mother was kind enough to take us early, so
we could lie on top of her car at the marina next to the airport,

and have a Wayne-and-Garth-AAAHH experience, while planes flew so close over us that we thought we would surely die each time. It was GREAT.

"Delia," Brady said between airplane encounters, "do you find Bugs Bunny attractive when he puts a dress on and pretends to be a girl?"

"Nooo," I said, "Noooo!" I added (just like Wayne, by the way—I could be his understudy, I'm so good at his lines). "And, see? You ARE Garth, Brady. That's his line."

She was about to push me off the car, but the next plane was coming in for a landing, so we went into our AAAAHHHH thing, which we freeze-framed in mid-AAAHHH for as long as we could, but then started laughing until we both rolled off the car.

We do amuse ourselves.

I called Giulio before we went to the airport, thinking that he might want to go with us, since almost getting hit by airplanes can really cheer a person up. But he said he still couldn't be with Brady, that it was too painful.

"I know Brady and I were only together for, uh, only about—"

"Fifty and a half days, approximately," I said, helping him out with the math.

"But it feels like a wound that will not heal if I see her," he said.

"Giulio, maybe it's just culture shock, because of the traveling and all, and you'll wake up tomorrow, and you'll feel fine, and you'll be ready to DEAL," I said, with an emphasis on the DEAL, which I hoped would make him think of DEEL, as in me, and it would have one of those unconscious (or is it called unbliminal?) advertising sorts of effects, and he'd wake up the next day and not be able to get his mind (or maybe even something else) off of me.

Well . . . could happen.

When we got to the airport, Tatyana and Noori were just arriving. It was neat to meet them, except for the part where they said, "So, Delia, what does it mean to be a 'Rogue'?"

(FaceBook. Bringing the planet together.)

Before I could (attempt to) explain about that, AJ came running up a nearby escalator and threw himself into Noori's arms. He was sobbing like a baby. It was quite a spectacle, which could only have been improved if Shakita had been there to witness it.

My mom had to drop me at the football field right from the airport, because Coach had called a special practice. I was very happy to get out of the car, since Noori and AJ were PDA-ing in the back seat. Surprisingly—but not surprisingly, from a PDA-avoidance standpoint—Brady and Tatyana jumped out of the car, too, and announced that they wanted to watch the practice.

Tatyana enjoyed meeting the football players—a little too

much, in my opinion. (Did I used to act like that before I settled down with my imaginary fulltime boyfriend?) She was especially impressed with Richard's shoulder pads.

"So, you have a 'friend' coming soon, I hear," I said, feeling a little troubled by her going on and on (with a maddeningly excellent sort of Britishish English) about her "lurve" of American football quarterbacks. "That tall, French-Vietnamese guy from the cruise, right?"

"He's not coming after all," she said. "He had a family thing, but I went to see him in Paris a few weeks ago."

"So, you're real attached, then?" I asked.

"Pals, actually. Cozy pals."

"What are cozy pals?" I asked (fearfully).

"You get, uh, COZY sometimes, like when you're watching a movie. Some snogging, maybe, but not really serious. I have several cozy pals."

I made a mental note to keep Giulio far, far away from this girl.

After the practice I had to go visit my X-Men for "final fittings," and I made Tatyana and Brady come with me. I have to say, these boys are skilled, and I am sure they will be very successful at getting into Parsons, which is their common goal, I have learned.

"It fits like a glove," Prof X said.

"It _is_ a glove," I said, holding up a yellow hand.

"I mean the whole package," he said. "You're stunning."

I looked in the full-length mirror they'd set up. I was wearing Spandex. Lots of Spandex. Yellow and green, mostly. Except for a silver belt made of fun foam.

"This will be the best Halloween ever!" Wolfie cried.

"I don't know what it is that really happens on Halloween," Tatyana said. "I've never seen one."

The boys looked at each other, smiled like little kids and began rummaging through a closet. Then they threw a black gown over Tatyana's head and fluffed around her for a minute or so and said, "Meet Mystique!"

"She's perfect!" Cyclops said.

"I lurve it!" Tatyana said, admiring herself in the mirror. "What am I, though?"

"You're one of us, honey, an X-Man," Wolfie said. "And looking good, too!"

"Oh, guys??" I said. "Little question: How come I didn't get a choice to wear the attractive, black gown instead of this lemon-lime thing?"

"Because you're the Rogue," Prof X said. "Duh."

I didn't know how to respond to that, so I chose not to.

"What should we use to make Mystique's skin blue?" Cyclops asked, his finger tapping his cheek.

"My what what?" Tatyana asked.

"Just say no," I whispered to her. "That's what we do in America, or else we get into trouble."

"Who's got the camera?" Magneto cried. "These will be great shots for the Parsons' portfolio!"

I may spend this Halloween looking a little weird (okay, a lot weird), but at least I will be in the company of goal-oriented people. My mother will be very proud.

Brady has a game tonight, and I have, by some miracle, convinced Giulio to go. He protested at first, saying, again, that he couldn't be close to Brady. But I pointed out that we could sit at the very back of the bleachers, and he'd be, like, miles away from her. (Or some distance or other.) Then he made the argument that he jinxes her, and I pointed out that she's been striking out plenty without him being there, so he obviously had nothing to do with her luck. Then he did his sad nodding thing and agreed to go with me.

There's a GO, and a WITH, and a ME, all in a row, there. Progress, yes?

Now my only worry is that the cruisers are going, too, which means Tatyana will be there. She's really nice, and I do like her, but she obviously can't be totally trusted around a person's guy.

Much the way I can't be totally trusted around a person's

guy, I guess, but we don't need to make EVERY connection that comes into our heads, now do we?

Tata!

cozy

Today, apparently, is the last day of the quarter and the last day we are keeping these "poetry" journals. When I asked the Colonel why he hadn't WARNED us about this, he had some lame excuse, like "I have announced it every day for two weeks." OutRAGEous that he would expect us to remember that.

I'll definitely have to do something really crazed and keep a personal journal of my own from now on, because I've become addicted to writing about interesting things, such as my own life. Which has—you will soon agree—gotten very, VERY, interesting all of a sudden. I believe it was Monday evening when the winds of change started blowing in, pushing up some dust from across the baseball field . . .

We started out with a five-person cheering section at Brady's game, which included me, Giulio, Tatyana, Noori, and AJ. Well, three people were cheering. AJ and Noori were acting the same as always. (I have forgotten what their faces look like.) Giulio and I got there before the others, so I suggested he sit at the end of a row, and I sat next to him, figuring that would be a great way to keep Tatyana from getting "cozy" ideas. But when she got there, she sat down behind him, which put her in a position to give him an occasional squeeze on the shoulders when she "thought he was looking too tense."

But other than that, everything was fine, and we were clapping and shouting and trying to help Brady get a hit. Every time the ball came sailing down from the mound it looked SO like she was going to slam the thing, and we'd all be holding our breath (although, AJ and Noori were holding their breath for a different reason), but the ball would suddenly turn invisible—as best I could tell—and the bat seemed to go RIGHT through it. This went on until the sixth inning, when something unexpected happened.

Brady got up to bat, and she missed the first pitch and missed the second pitch (swinging so hard she almost knocked herself down) and then the third pitch reached the plate, and she hit it, HARD. She started to run, and we watched as it just barely hit outside the right field foul line. There was this loud OHHH sound from the team, and Brady, who had made it all the way to second base, started to trot back along the baseline. The ball— because it had so much power on it—continued to bounce and went out of the playing area and rolled up to the feet of someone who was just arriving at the game. It was Richard. And he scooped up the ball, tossed it to the right fielder, and gave Brady (who had stopped and was looking at him with a strange

164

expression) a smile and a thumbs-up.

She sent the next pitch so far over the outfield fence that no one even bothered going to look for it. And the next time she was up: SAME. And last time she was up: SAME.

There was a lot of cheering the rest of the game. AJ and Noori even got into it, yelling and stomping. And Giulio was cheering, but I could tell it made him feel weird that Richard seemed to be the person who had brought Brady the luck. So when the game ended, Giulio left quickly, before she came out of the dugout.

And when she did, she hugged us one by one (which, by the expressions on Tatyana's and Noori's faces, grossed them out as much as it grosses me out, thank-you-very-much), and when she got to Richard, she definitely gave him a hug that was longer than the rest of ours.

Which made me feel very PRICKLY, again, because (I figured) it seemed awfully soon after Giulio that she was giving an extended-type hug to another guy. But, of course, I would have done the same, given the opportunity with Giulio, so I told myself to just stop feeling that way, and GET OVER IT. I didn't really listen to myself, though, because I felt that way right up until the Halloween party last night, when those winds of change organized themselves into a full-blown twister . . .

Tatyana and I arrived at the community center with the other X-Men half an hour after the party started, because they wanted to "make a splash." Tatyana and I were planning to dance together as soon as we got there, but the song was really slow, so we decided to wait for a faster one. We noticed, right away, AJ and Noori swaying close by (both in cowboy hats and western shirts, and judging by how adorably big these things were on Noori, I'm guessing she'd borrowed these items from AJ).

The next song turned out to be slow, too, and Tatyana decided to go dance with Magneto, so I stood there, doing nothing, dressed in all my Spandex. Then, IT HAPPENED. There was a tap on my shoulder, and Giulio was suddenly THERE, smiling his beautiful, Italian smile. And he said:

"You were right, Delia. It was just culture shock! And I am all better now, and I have realized that I am not in love with Brady. Will you dance with me?"

So we drifted onto the dance floor, and we were dancing slow and close, and he was saying all the right things to me (like that I was incredibly funny and exceptionally gorgeous), and he was just the right height for me and just the right build, and everything was JUST SO RIGHT.

Until I got another tap on the shoulder, and it was Brady. And she said, "I've changed my mind, Delia. I need Giulio back."

And I shook my head and said, "Nooo," and she nodded her head, and said, "Yesss," and we went back and forth with this for a while, and then she started wrestling me, and we accidentally knocked over a spotlight that was lighting up the dance floor, and it burst into flames, and soon the entire ROOM was on fire, and, and—

Okay, hit the pause button.

As IF I would let things end THAT way. Come on!

For the MEGA-TRUE-ENDING, rewind to the part where I'm standing alone, after Tatyana goes off with Magneto . . .

Prof X rolled up next to me (having found a wheelchair, it seems) and asked if I would like to dance.

"I don't think so," I said.

"I have telepathic powers," he said.

"That's really cool and all, but it's not YOU, it's the wheelchair," I said. "It'll kill my shins."

Shakita appeared at that moment (in a Hillary Clinton mask) and began scolding me for discriminating against the handicapped.

"But he's not handicapped," I said.

"Then why is he in a wheelchair?" she asked.

"I'm paraplegic due to an accident involving the alien, Lucifer," he said, rolling off in a huff.

"Being paraplegic is definitely a handicap," Shakita said to me.

Luckily, we were distracted then by the arrival of a short guy who walked like a robot and parked himself directly in front of me. He had a <u>Star</u> <u>Trek</u> T-shirt on and was wearing Dr. Spock ears.

"You're a Trekkie!" Shakita said to him. "My dad's a Trekkie!"

"I am Gorkon," he said.

"Gorkon!" I repeated.

"I just found out about the party 2.6 hours ago, IMing with Brady. As it turns out, my personal coordinates are very near. However, I did not have time to get a costume," he said, still standing exactly in front of me with the top of his head about at my chin level, and the tips of his pointy ears at my, eh, chest level.

"Hm," I said, trying to slowly slide away from him, unnoticed.

"Which is your favorite <u>Star</u> <u>Trek</u> episode?" Shakita asked him.

"Number 306, Spock's Brain," he said.

"I LOVE that one!" she cried. "Come on, you've got to dance with me!"

And she pulled him off to the dance floor, and I was alone again, so I went to the snack table to do some munching. There, I found Giulio. He was sitting on a stool and was wearing a long black cape that was dramatically bunched up on the floor around him, and he had a paintbrush behind one ear and was drawing in a sketchpad.

"Let me guess," I said. "You're a Renaissance artist."

"Yes, that's right," he said, and I noticed his sunny, Italian smile had returned. "I want to thank you, Delia, because I am feeling so much better after the things you said to me. I am glad we are friends. I will not be having any more American girlfriends, because I need to be working hard on my art now."

I stood, waiting to feel the impact of this news. A garbage truck dropped from ten stories up and landing on my head is the sort of feeling I expected, so I braced myself.

Tatyana wandered over to the snack table while I was waiting for the truck to hit me, and she peeked over Giulio's shoulder at his sketch pad. "Oooh! You are good," she said to him, doing that shoulder-squeezing-thing again. "Can you draw me?"

"I will be delighted," he said.

And Tatyana sat on a stool and looked very pretty in her black and silver gown, and I watched all this and waited to get crushed to a yellow pulp, but you know what? It never happened. I wasn't upset. Even when Tatyana said something about feeling very "cozy" there, I WASN'T upset.

Then that "Magic Carpet Ride" song started, and I looked out at the dance floor. My eye immediately landed on Brady, who was dressed in her baseball uniform (washed, thankfully), and she was dancing and talking with someone in a football uniform (also washed, thankfully), and I was peering at them to see which one of my teammates was there at the party, and that's when I saw that it was Richard. And I got that PRICKLY feeling again, only it was MAJOR this time, like I'd just been wrestling with a porcupine.

And I realized at that moment why Giulio had not been the garbage truck. It was because RICHARD was the garbage truck. (Speaking metaphorifically.) And I also realized then that I had a brand new problem, and it seemed to be, actually, the exact same problem I'd had to start with.

So I stood there, alone again in Spandex, and watched some couples who seemed to be having a good time—Shakita and Gorkon (a perfect match, but for no reason that makes any sense), AJ and Noori (the only people I know who can slow dance to a fast song)—and I wished I were them. Well, not exactly THEM, but people with other people they really like, you know? And I was feeling all sorry for myself, and my head was saying these sorts of things to me:

Richard?? How did this happen? And WHEN did this happen? Well, it happened NOW, of course, but how did I not see it coming? RICHARD??

Luckily—before the voices took over completely—Magneto appeared in front of me, the shiny medals that covered his chest all glistening in the light from the disco ball that had started spinning at the beginning of the song. "Let's dance," he said.

In my weakened state, I followed him onto the dance floor. When we found a spot in the middle, I guess I reached out to grab his hand (as normal people sometimes DO when they're dancing), but he jerked it back and said, "Don't touch!"

"Uh, sorry," I said.

"It's your powers," he explained.

"I have powers?" (This was news.)

"Rogue absorbs the strength of others," he said. "So you have just taken a bit of my magnetic power from me with that touch."

"Whoa," I said.

"I'm sorry to inform you in this way," he said. "I didn't realize you were clueless about that."

"CLUELESS, yes, that describes my situation well," I said, seeing the back of Richard just a few couples away from us. Brady was whispering something to him. And then she was smiling and laughing and whispering again.

"You can be very dangerous," Magneto said. "And you should know there is more—"

But he was interrupted then by Brady, who suddenly appeared in front of him and began dancing.

"Let's switch!" she said, and I got pushed in the direction of

Richard, which caused me to run right into him.

"Sorry!" I said, stepping back, laughing (snorting, actually) and trying to continue dancing, all casual-like. "I just absorbed some magnetic power, and I guess I don't know how to use it yet."

"Yeah, you're Rogue," he said. "I know what you can do to a person."

"You do?" I asked.

"I was really into X-Men when I was a kid. I was a major game geek."

"I remember that. You used to come to my house."

The song stopped right about then, and the next one started. It was "Imagine" by John Lennon, which is the slowest song known to man. You can imagine (hehe) the discomfort I was expecting over this particular dance situation, what with all my new-found feelings for Richard, and not knowing yet the details of his status with Brady. But then Richard—very boldly, and un-Richard-like— put his hands on my hips (er, Rogue belt). So I put my hands on his shoulders (er, shoulder pads).

"You do know," I said, trying to sound very cool and calm, but my voice insisted on coming out a little too high-pitched, "that by the end of this dance you could have NO physical strength at all?"

"I believe that," he said, laughing. And I could feel his laugh against my ear, which is a most sensitive place, and so my head found itself nestling rather comfortably against his neck. (Not my fault—obviously the magnets I'd just absorbed.)

"You know why I used to go to your house?" he asked me.

"I have wondered that," I said.

"Well, it was because I was so in love with you when I was little. Brady told me I should tell you about that."

Figuring it might be part of some clearing-the-air-to-start-going-out thing between the two of them, I said, "True confessions, huh? Anything else I need to know?"

"Yeah," he said (and I could feel that body-temp-spiking he gets, which suddenly seemed a not-so-unattractive quality). "I still feel that way. Actually."

And then, the magnets I'd swallowed (or whatever it was I did with them) got suddenly, uncontrollably strong, and I could feel myself getting closer and closer to him.

"That's why I joined the football team," he went on. "I figured, since you wanted to be the manager that you like that type of guy."

"Oh, I don't," I said.

"Oh," he said.

"I mean, I thought I didn't like the football type. But I guess I do now. Or one in particular. Tu."

"You like two in particular?"

"No, one."

"But didn't you just say two?"

"Tu is Italian for 'you.'"

"Me?" he said, and his voice cracked in a very cute, shy, deer-Richard-ish way.

"Coach is NOT going to be happy about this," I said. "What with this power I've got and all."

"What really worries me is your OTHER power," he said.

"I've got another power?" I asked.

"Yeah, when Rogue kisses someone, he dies."

And then (cue end of song) we stood looking at each other until I said, "Bummer for you," and—

Oops! That's the bell.

Arrivederci!